Published by Ad Hoc Fiction.
www.AdHocFiction.com

Purchasing Information:
Paperback available from www.AdHocFiction.com
E-book available from all usual outlets.

Printed in the United Kingdom.
First printing 2025.

ISBN paperback 978-1-915247-66-7
ISBN e-Book 978-1-915247-67-4

The Constancy of Woodpigeons

Bath Flash Fiction Volume Nine

AdHoc Fiction

Foreword

We're pleased to introduce *The Constancy of Woodpigeons*, the ninth anthology from the Bath Flash Fiction Award, published by Ad Hoc Fiction, containing 137 flash fictions of 300 words and under, by authors from the three Awards in 2024. We received, in total, 2948 entries, again from over 40 countries:

Australia, Austria, Belgium, Bulgaria, Brazil, Cambodia, Canada, Chile, Croatia, Cyprus Czech Republic, Denmark, France, Georgia, Germany, Greece, Hong Kong, Hungary, India, Ireland, Italy, Japan, Jersey, Luxembourg, Malta, Mauritius, Mexico, Morocco, Netherlands, New Zealand, Nigeria, Norway, Philippines, Poland, Singapore, South Africa, Spain, Sri Lanka, Sweden, Switzerland, Taiwan, United Arab Emirates, United Kingdom, United States, Vietnam.

Thank you very much to everyone who entered. Each long list of fifty stories was sent anonymously to an independent judge to choose a short list of twenty and the five winning stories.

This year, the three judges for the Awards were Susmita Bhattacharya from the UK (February); Michelle Elvy from New Zealand (June); Matt Kendrick from the UK (October). All the judges are very experienced writers, editors and writing teachers. We very much appreciated their careful consideration of the stories. They wrote excellent reports and included thoughtful, specific comments on the winners. Their reports can be read in full on our website, bathflashfictionaward.com. Brief extracts from these reports are below:

For the February Award, Susmita wrote:

"I'm in awe of the flash fiction pieces I read, the idea, the crafting of the story, the structure and how these stories got such a variety of reactions from me. A sharp intake of breath, a few tears, a nodding of the head, a smile..."

For the June Award, Michelle Elvy wrote:

"This was a rich set of flash fictions, and they required reading several times before the ones that stuck started to emerge – because so many were memorable. I have so enjoyed considering the many virtues of all of them."

For the October Award, Matt Kendrick wrote:

"Flash fiction presents such a wide range of possibilities in terms of narrative, character, tone and form, and the writers of these pieces have made full use of these."

The fifteen placed stories from the three Awards are at the beginning of the book, followed by the remainder of the short list (judges' selections) and the rest of the long listed stories (editors' choices). The contents list of titles is at the beginning and an index at the end matches page numbers to authors' stories. Pick and choose, or read straight through. They are all wonderful examples of flash fiction.

Publication has been delayed due to unforeseen circumstances this year, and we're very appreciative of the production editor at Ad Hoc Fiction, for his work to publish it now. Thank you to all contributors for their patience in waiting to see their stories published.

This year, the title story, 'The Constancy of Woodpigeons', is by writer Tracy Fells from the UK. It is a moving story, with an unresolved ending, and we love the title and the way Tracy uses the metaphor of the pigeons to show how suddenly life can change. This story is about the possible end of a long relationship, but we think it also shows the precariousness of the world.

We look forward to reading more wonderful flash fictions on all subjects in the 2025 Awards and producing our 10th flash fiction anthology.

Jude Higgins
Founder, Bath Flash Fiction Award
May, 2025

Contents

Kathryn Aldridge-Morris

Visiting Lenin's Tomb

Tiyshe! No talking! The soldiers put fingers purple with cold to their cracked lips. You are here to pay homage! Da zdravstvuyet Leninizm! But this is your ex-husband's house, not the dim lit mausoleum on Red Square, and those guards, eyes the colour of dill, mouths downturned sickles, your daughters. How they've changed but not changed since you were disappeared, and he threatened to section you, should you ever return. Exiled to the end of the Piccadilly Line, sixteen stops away from their entire childhood. *Move along! Dvigatsya!* You want to slow, to take in the red granite walls, the unfamiliar family photos, the smell of wet overcoat, but a celebrant with cyrillic curls for a moustache tells you to wait outside, it's for the best, they don't want a scene, and as you reach Lenin's tomb — some honeymoon—you don't yet know you're shuffling through the few remaining days of Gorbachev's Russia. You oblige and stand in the snow, but your nerves are in insurrection. How dare this stranger—yet another man—stand between you and your daughters? You grip the letters you'll give them today, letters to you from their father, letters that prove the mind-games and control; control over what you wore, where you went, who you saw. You *were* a good mother! You did *try* to see them! The hearse pulls up, his coffin flanked by the floral tribute he picked out himself: BEST DAD. A crowd swells at the foot of Gorky Street. In weeks a drunk will climb on top of a tank to declare a new era, but for now your daughters turn their backs on you, light Kino cigarettes and leave iron blue contrails that dissipate in the cold Essex air.

Mairead Robinson

A Palimpsest of Cheerleaders

Mel's in the bleachers, inspecting her shattered shin-bone, pantyhose around her ankles, thighs like a pair of suckling pigs. Sadie reckons Mel would've been crowned, but I think Sadie herself; even with her stomach bleeding out, she has that poise, that prom-queen pout. 'Why d'you even care?' I say, 'We're dead, remember?'

'*Posthumously*,' she snaps. Her tear-brim gaze moves beyond Mel, and I know she's seeing the blue silk draped wraith-like on its hanger, the strappy shoes, the simple silver locket. I've seen her touching fingers to the hollow of her throat, mouthing, 'Me?'

The field's Elysium green. *Palimpsest*. Miss Ingram chalked it on the board; *a parchment erased, marks beneath still visible*; squeak of plimsols on the locker room floor, jocks charging out, ball flying high, crowd on their feet, and us, mid-routine, twizzling pom-poms on the T-stretch, hearts wide open to Danny Markham's bullets as he riddled the squad, taking us all out.

Mel was sweet on Danny, mistook dark-eyed hatred for love-sick brooding, and hoped for his corsage on prom night. 'Fat chance,' says Sadie as she lunges, hands on hips, elbows out. I joined because Mom said college, and who knew cheerleading scholarships were a thing? So, there I was, and here I am, effaced by kite-high Danny, his Pa's M16 spitting fire. *He was troubled*, wailed Mel, blasted leg a right angle, fatal bullet lodged in her heart like Cupid's flinty arrowhead.

Shadow-shapes stand in the dug-outs. Our mothers, so small, wispy as smoke. Mel hops over and suggests we do the lead-in, so we're high-kicking, pike jumping, pom-poms razzle-dazzling as we holler the chant, as if they could hear us, as if we could scribe ourselves anew beneath the yearbook obituaries, as if there was anything left save all this ache, this longing.

Sara Hills

A Cock Among the Bathers

Tomorrow at the Tate Modern, while she's studying Cézanne's bathers, Jake will take off his pants. Jake, who's old enough to know that public indecency's a crime, old enough, sure — but still young enough to be stupid, reckless because he thinks he's in love, thinks he can win her over if he makes a scene. And before she can grab his arm and say *Jake, stop!* he'll have already left his smalls on the wooden floor, and he'll stand full buck with arms outstretched, trying to achieve, *well... bathing*, she'll guess, like one of Cézanne's malformed women, oyster-white with willowed backs and tree-trunked hips, except Jake's not a woman — he's told her as much, said she can't keep crying her heartbreaks, oppressing him with her problems unless she's willing to see him as more. And of course she knows he's a man, it's his performance schtick she can't take — his spotlighting, pushing, trying too hard — like tomorrow, at the Tate, when he'll slip from his smalls before gobble-eyed children and gasping mothers with eye-covering hands, before men muttering *Mate, you can't!* and *What in God's name!* and Jake's grin, his pearlescent grin! and his outstretched arms and his fur-tufted ass, cleft as a Cézannesque peach, and the *Sir! Sir!* from the gallery attendants and the neon security-ites with their walkie-talkies and Jake's eyes pleading, pleading for her to see it as more than a scene, as a shared story, an anecdote for later, when they can say *Remember the time at the Tate?* like it's enough of a something, and though he'll be singing as they drag him away, tufted cleft in retreat, something falsetto or operatic about love, about water, second chances and firsts, the heat of her hand still echoing on his arm, despite herself, goddammit, she'll laugh.

Emily Rinkema

Driving my Seven-Year Old Nephew to Visit His Mother at Rehab

It's his turn, and from the back seat he tosses out an easy one. "Would you rather eat a mile of garbage or a mile of worms?" I make eye contact through the mirror, ask some follow-ups: how fat are the worms? Fat. Are they alive? Yes. Would I have to eat everything in the garbage, or just the food-ish things? Everything, he says.

"Easy," I say. "Worms."

It's a game we've been playing together since he could talk, since he started spending nights at my apartment, since he learned about worst case scenarios that didn't involve choice.

I give him one I've been saving: "Would you rather drink a cup of your own pee, or half a cup of a stranger's pee?"

He squeals. "My pee," he says, and then, "Gross!"

We are a few minutes away now. I slow the car and turn onto an unmarked road. The first few times here we drove right past. When we get there, I'll wait outside while he sits on a couch across from my sister, supervised, and she'll cry and ask him questions that all end with the word me. He'll spend the two-hour drive home silent and I will hate her for it, then hate myself for hating her, unsure which is worse.

"My turn," he says, his voice low. "Would you rather have me live with you forever or have your arm chopped off with an axe?"

"Another easy one," I say. I wink at him in the mirror, but he's looking out the window. He looks just like her. I wonder which would hurt more, the blade severing the limb, or the moment just after, when you realize what's been done.

Jo Withers

All The Things That We Are Not

The soldiers came quickly, took us to the shelter (not a house, not a home). Said we'd be safe here (not happy). Inside, women and children (not men, not husbands, not brothers, not fathers) huddled together (not together, in the same space).

We're all the same now (not people). It had always happened somewhere else before (not real, not us).

We knew each other by our clothes (not names) what we were wearing when the bombs fell (not like snow, not like tears). Some in business suits, some in school uniform; a waitress in her coffee-stained apron, a baker with flour splattered up her arm (not white, dotted red with blood).

We ran into the streets at the sound of the explosions, torn from our past lives (not present, not future, gone). The sky filled with smoke (not birds, not clouds, not sun). We ran from the explosions and the screams (not away, just further, still heard, still haunting).

They pulled us into trucks, drove us to safety (not sure, not certain). Took us to the bunker with no windows (not night, not day) gave us water and food. We were grateful although we were cold and scared because at least we were here (not outside, not captured, not dead).

Yesterday we were at work, at school, at home (not cocooned weeping in the dark). If today was like every day before (not shredded, not eviscerated, not annulled) I would meet my sister after work. Her office was south of the city where the damage was worst (not hopeful, not likely) and whole streets were now gaping holes (not pathways, not roads) and although the soldiers return every hour, bringing more people, reuniting family and friends, each time the door opens they are strangers (not her, not her, not her).

Alys Hobbs

There you are

You wake in the carpark of a long-forgotten Little Chef. In the chain-link there are clumps of things that once had feathers and tails and chickweed is coming up through the cracks in the concrete. You wake in a layby. You wake in a cul-de-sac to a hob-knuckled rapping, but no-one is there when you open the door. You wake in a Stopping Place. You wake at the edge of a bare-plucked field with your neck in a knot, forgetting where you were. Sometimes when you try to sleep among the sweet-sour smell of yourself you pretend it's not cars rushing by but the ocean rushing in, picking you up, bearing you off. You wake by a reservoir and rain is falling or the trees are shedding their needles in the coming of winter or someone is tapping, tapping on the roof, calling you out. In a drive-thru bin you purge your flotsam; the cans, the tins, the clusters, the clods; the dried-out wet-wipes, the gummed-up noodle cups, the buttons and bones and bottle caps. You wake in the crook of the woods, your fingers working deep under the seat-covers like you're digging for something buried in the damp. You wake in a Welcome Break and the moon is a hot-white hangnail and you taste salt in the split where your mouth used to be. You wake by a lakeside. You've been here before. You wake in the quiet. You'll go here again. You wake in the thin light to the sound of geese leaving. The windows are so fogged with your own breath that you can't look out, but you think it must really be something to see.

Gayathiri Dhevi Appathurai

How to make a realistic Paper Rose

First, you can choose what colour and type of rose you want to make.
~~My father would disagree; after all, he didn't want a girl, but what choice did he have with me?~~

Take a sheet of paper. It should be flexible but not too delicate.
~~My mother would disagree; a girl should be delicate, or else what would the family think of her upbringing?~~

Cut 3 squares of that paper, even 4. Size doesn't matter. The bigger, the better.
~~My parents would disagree; girls can never have a big ego. So why give them so much learning?~~

Take one square and fold diagonally, repeat two more folds, making it small.
~~My grandma would disagree; a woman shouldn't feel small to obey a man. Isn't that how we preserve family values?~~

Draw an arc, cut the top, and a little at the bottom. You get a creased flower shape with a hole, but it isn't complete yet.
My family would disagree; marriage completes a woman. What really does ~~a solitary life accomplish?~~

Curl the edges of a flower, cut one pie shape, and glue the open edges together like a cone; one segment remains untethered.
~~My husband would disagree; a woman must be tethered to her man's will. How else can marriage work?~~

Repeat steps 4 through 6 for other squares, cutting one segment more each time. You get smaller flower cones and more segments separated.
~~My family would disagree; separation is never a choice. Why would a man hit his woman unless she angered him?~~

Curl and make cones out of the lone segments. Assemble from largest to smallest cones and adjust until the flower looks whole.
~~My parents would agree. A woman must always adjust. No more questions.~~

Finally, this is it. You are done.
~~I agree.~~

Samantha Kent

There are times when we talk without talking

Her nieces arrive first. All three of them, mid-twenties, clad in looping scarves and the guilt of being absent since their mid-teens.

Then her son, his eyes trained on the notices pinned to the walls, on the white rectangle of sky out the window. His pregnant wife, his pretty daughters, their vitality as sharp and painful as a knife.

Finally her husband, back from pacing the sterile corridors. Knuckles white, eyes red, fingers tobacco yellow.

The room is warm – nauseating – but her feet, she says, are cold.

One by one her visitors ask if she'd like another blanket. One by one they are informed by the others, in jovial tones, that she already has three, ten, a thousand.

Over her dying body – because it is dying, now, the doctors are sure – the visitors draw a line around the thing they can't face talking about and take a step further back for good measure.

You're how old? Wow. How's big school treating you?

That's frustrating. Do you think your buyers will stick around?

No time off in between jobs, no. If only!

They loved it. They're definitely cruise people now.

He's good. Just hungover, or he would have come along too.

Every now and then the visitors force themselves to look down at the woman propped up against the pillows, to return her slumped and crooked smile.

It is easy to wonder how she might be feeling, beyond the icy feet and the aching lungs and the wounds from the failed cannula. But it is hard – it is impossible – to ask.

In time, snow begins to fall, and conversation turns to the weather.

Catherine Ogston

On Friday Nights in May I Sit Quietly with a Friend

The faerie man is sitting next to me, just like last Friday and the one before that, while forest insects buzz and flit and the evening sunlight touches the nodding bluebell heads. So many dogs he mutters, as yet another runs past the signs telling their owners to keep them on a leash. A man walks on the path, a tripod and Cyclops-eyed camera tucked under one arm, followed by another. How about one of them, the faerie asks and I wrinkle my nose. The faerie hands me a bluebell and tells me that turning it inside out will win me the heart of my true love and so I try peeling the soft trumpet-headed petals but they tear like damp paper and fall groundward. Better keep practising, he tells me although we both know the heavy-scented flowers are about to sink down into the forest floor for another year. Last week the man versus bear debate came up and before I had completed my explanation the faerie man told me, with unsettling adamance, to always choose the bear. In his nimble fingers the delicate petals bend and fold obediently. Your sweetheart's name starts with M he says and I sigh, ask him to do another one because I've had it with Marks and Mikes and Martins. No do-overs he tells me and we go back to sitting in silence, only the whisper of the leaves and ferns in our ears. One of the photographers strides past and the faerie says, maybe he is M and I reply that maybe he is a worse option than the bear. How can you tell asks the faerie and I agree, how can you ever, ever tell?

Sarah Gillett

An experiment on a bird in the airpump

(after Joseph Wright of Derby)

Anna so wanted to stroke its soft white body that she poked her fingers into the cage when Maria wasn't looking. The cockatoos tabbed, drawing blood with its curved beak, tongue waggling. They both screamed and it went back to preening itself, nibbling under its downy parts, closing its wings with a dry snap, smoothing down its combed head with grey claws. Maria said she deserved to get pecked, it wasn't a pet and if anything happened to it then Papa would be filthy angry and likely lock her in the box under the stairs until they all forgot she was there, until she died. Anna, yelling, wished she could be a ghost and haunt Mariaf orever and ever and always. Shrieking then giggling they washed their faces and fumbled each other into pale lilac silk dresses.

Downstairs the parlour table was set with wooden instruments, connected by brass tubing, polished handles, glass vessels. When Anna asked Papa what the gnarled slimy thing in the amber liquid was, he said it was a diseased human skull. The sisters shivered. Papa's important friend placed the cockatoo inside a large glass jar and demonstrated the effects of something called a vacuum, counting seconds on a silver watch.

The white bird shone in the candlelight. It looked fragile and heavy, its feathers wide, its feet scrabbling then twitching slower. Maria hid her face but Anna could not look away. She wanted to touch the glossy black eye staring right at her. Around her, moving splashes of cheek and hair and cloth caught the light in time with the thumping of her heart. She had thought it was only in the shadows that everything was dark and treacherous. Time was slower there, the box had taught her that. She held her breath and waited.

R. V. Jones

The Bee

The bee that will kill John Smith rises from a flower. To this flower and the next, the bee is an angel, a miracle.

Had today been a Friday, John Smith would have stayed in, poured a small sherry, listened to Radio Four. He might have thought about various chores, admin, accounts…

But today is magnificent, and so will be John's death. But John does not know this or understand. He does not hear angels or that distant buzz, for he is but a man, and when angels speak, man is deaf and blind.

Once, when John was barely twenty-one, he dreamed of Alice, the girl then who is now the woman of the house. Alice sits inside, vaguely hearing the radio, the hum of the sun.

Through their engagement, they pretended they would never tire of each other, and that almost came to pass, even if both strayed the once, each pausing on a petal that seemed so lovely. In hindsight, two mistakes.

Hindsight says, "I told you so", but hindsight lies. It is not hindsight that John lacked or Alice lacks, but vision, understanding a larger picture.

John's son languishes in Maidstone Prison and this tiny prick will release him. And John and Alice have a daughter, Jennifer, a thin girl with certain difficulties who thinks of naked clowns and weeps constantly, but this insect kiss, the bee's soft touch, will change everything, the clowns will leave her, and Jennifer will come home.

To the flower the bee is impossible, a droning 747, carrying a kiss of love. Now comes its greatest, happy, auspicious moment.

Alice drifts; light glints on the Harveys. John opens the shed, the lawnmower gleams. The bee enters the garden.

Gemma Church

Godetias

Eight letters.

I'd never heard of GODETIAS until I started listening to *Countdown*. Never watched it neither cos I was at school… or bunking off, if you want the truth.

Anyway, two contestants (complete nerds) pick nine random letters. Then, they've got to get the longest word in 30 seconds while the *Countdown* clock ticks down.

Sounds dumb, right? But I've learned loads of new words.

GODETIAS comes up a lot cos certain letter combos are more likely.

ASTEROID.

RODENTIA.

ORDINATE.

Eight letters.

Popular and anagrams of each other.

FAVOURITE.

Nine letters.

Claire's the favourite. She's smart. Went to uni. Left me with…

RELATIONS.

The most popular niner.

PHYSICIAN.

Nine letters but rare.

They came into my room today, RELATIONS and PHYSICIAN.

I was annoyed cos they turned the TV off.

PHYSICIAN spewed out loads of (nine-plus) words that I couldn't understand. I stopped listening, cos I was pissed about missing the end of *Countdown.*

When PHYSICIAN left, RELATIONS started arguing. Again.

The worst thing was, I had to lie here, listening to the same old...

BULLSHIT.

Eight letters.

Countdown allows swear words, if they're in the dictionary.

VEGETABLE.

Niner. Not popular. What RELATIONS called me.

But they're wrong. I'm still in here and I've found something I'm good at and I'm going to go on *Countdown* and prove that I'm no…

WASTER.

Six letters. Crap Countdown word. But everyone's FAVOURITE word to describe me.

Want to know the worst bit about lying here?

Claire hasn't visited.

That's hit me hard.

Harder than when Claire blocked me on her socials.

But not as hard as the tree that I drove RELATIONS' car into.

I just wanted someone to see me.

Now, I'm trapped in my head.

Listening to *Countdown.*

Praying Claire visits and, maybe, brings me a bunch of GODETIAS.

Hannah Retallick

He Owed Me

When he died the man owed me £35 in petty cash and that was my first thought when I heard about The Accident, a collision between a camper van and lorry on the A55 which proved fatal for both drivers, the lorry man being the one who owed me £35, a twinkly-eyed neighbour, a single forty-something-year-old called Luca who smelt of cigarettes and bacon and always told me he loved my hair like that, like however it happened to be, up down blonde curly red straight black crimped, and we were starting to know each other quite well because he had got into the habit of rushing up to my front door and saying he needed to borrow some change to give as pocket money to his niece or for carpark tickets or for slot machines, so I would do the neighbourly thing and pluck coins from the dusty dish in my hallway, saying, 'Here, hope that helps', not knowing if I'd ever get it back but making a mental tally as though I needed to know how grateful he should be to me, and it was the selfishness of my first thought when I heard he'd died that meant I couldn't bear to go to his funeral, crumbling under the weight of guilt, because £35 doesn't matter in the face of death, and as the weeks passed I purged those thoughts completely and stopped torturing myself about the petty debt and my own failings and just wished I could ask Luca whether he really did love my hair like that, like however it happened to be, or whether he meant something else.

Pilar García Claramonte

Four Conditions of the Heart

-0-

Doctors are avoiding the zero conditional. No-one tells me, "*If a brain is deprived of oxygen for twelve minutes, it never recovers fully.*"

You sleep. I watch. We share this arctic cubicle with the beep and whirr of machines. One shivering certainty rises stark-naked with your in-breath and falls in time with your chest: *If you die, I die. If you die, I die.*

-1-

Fourteen days since you collapsed on our kitchen floor. Doctors use the first conditional daily now: "If your partner doesn't wake soon, we'll need to make decisions."

Your first conditionals were much easier.

If I promise coffee in bed forever, will you marry me?

If it's a girl, we'll name her Daisy.

If we retire next year, we'll grow old by the sea.

-2-

It's been thirty-two days. I hold your hand in one hand and write, with the other, the probable results of hypothetical situations. The complexity of the second conditional, scribbled on the back of hospital leaflets, is my foothold through this labyrinth.

If you woke, you would live significantly impaired, physically and mentally.

If you lived, you would not manage to breathe on your own.

At the end of the day, I scatter scraps of leaflets amongst binned paper cups. Acrid coffee coats my tongue across the dark drive home.

If you spoke, I know what you would tell me to do.

-3-

I tackle the third conditional in the classroom. The hardest of the four.

"You have to imagine the probable result of something unreal, impossible, something that didn't actually happen," I explain.

I write on the whiteboard: *If, eighteen months ago, he had lived …*

I pause, marker pen in the air. "In this conditional, there's often a sense of regret."

I wipe the board and start another sentence.

RJ Dwyer

Prognosis

You start by saying sorry.

"A tumour?" he asks, and you agree. He studies his palms. The collar of his shirt is stained, while the woman next door sports a perfect white cardigan. He brings her laundry, and they all say – what a catch. When she goes, he won't be long after. A hammering sound travels in through the window, and you raise your voice over it. When he meets your eye, he's on the verge of tears and you feel satisfied. It doesn't matter as much what's said now; he won't remember the details. He leans towards you, too close, and you correct the distance. When he asks if she's dying, you pause. Your heart beats too fast. It's almost exciting when you don't know which way they'll go. He might fall to his knees. Or hit you. He could even shrug and say, no worries.

He tells you that she loved to swim – how from the shore he would watch her head rise and fall among the black rocks. Once, a cut on the sole of her foot, and patches of blood left on the sand.

He tells you of the loss of their baby.

He tells you how he always felt, deep down, that she never really loved him quite as much.

How some days now she calls him by another name and looks at him differently.

How he usually goes along with this, all the same.

Later, you stop outside her room. The woman is sleeping, and he's hunched over the bed. For a moment, you think you see him holding a pillow to her face. He has one hand on her chest and with the other he runs a small comb over her fringe. You stand back from the glass, trying to make yourself small.

Gillian O'Shaughnessy

D Block at the Sacred Heart Maternity Hospital for Women and Children

She lies splayed and awkward on your chest, staring like she knows you're barely out of school. The vernix that warmed her in your womb is pearl-thick, she's pink as sin and skinny. You hold her too carefully, like a doll you think you might break. They peel her from your arms, you don't want to let go. They think you brought this on yourself, they think babies shouldn't have babies. You ask for your mother, and they tell you again she's not coming. You don't ask for your father.

They send you to the shower to wash and change. It's tiled in dull green; the water is lukewarm. There are no cubicles, or curtains, only a low wooden bench on which to place your wash bag, empty except for a toothbrush and paste, and a cake of cracked yellow soap you stole from the toilets at a petrol station. You are naked, blood drips in rivulets and clots from between your legs, it lands in fat crimson splatters on the floor. You feel like a beast in an abattoir. You don't know where they've taken your baby or when they'll bring her back.

In D Block you are far from the private rooms, proud parents, and powdered bundles snug as bugs in hand-stitched blankets. There are no flowers or cards or teddy bears fighting for room on the nightstand, no visitors to usher out at rest time. Your daughter lies in a trolley beside you, in a nappy frayed at the edges. Despite the clamour of the ward, she is sleeping, arms flung wide, small hands curled like spring ferns. She looks nothing like your father. You shift slightly closer, try to remember how it feels to breathe.

Linda Grierson-Irish

Rory's Fishing Tackle Shop

Whenever our cat didn't return home, we'd play the game. He's gone to check on his shop in Ireland, we'd say. There he'll be, chewing through the accounts, fixing the little tinkling doorbell, barbing his claws on ageing jambs.

We made Ina his main customer. It was far enough away to be possible. Near enough to feel true. How she loved the little trays of lures and flies, the regiments of rods and reels. We'd considered vintage clothing first, then crystals, stationery. Fishing tackle seemed appropriate, you said, because of how wide her eyes were when she asked "Daddy, do fish want to be caught?"

Rory would always canoodle back, fresh and faintly fragrant, his whiskers aquiver. We drilled him for shop news. He was knowledgeable, thanks to Ina. Even as a child she could distinguish between spinners, jigs, streamers. Rory brought us gifts – worms, maggots – but we persuaded him they weren't necessary. It was enough that he came home.

Then we overstepped the mark. We asked, 'How did she seem?' 'Were her eyes still as blue?' We fetched out photos of him mittening her lap. He said, "I'm a cat, I don't concern myself with such particulars."

Afterwards, you ran a Google search, jabbing to preserve the possible in our make-believe, and there it was. Rory's Fishing Tackle Shop in Dublin. For *real*. I stared at the photos, at the duffle-coated people coming and going. None of them was Ina. I hated those people. They probably bypassed have-you-seen posters every day, distracted by bait-filled pockets.

We stopped playing the game. I couldn't put Ina in a real shop, with solid walls and locks. And Rory wanders less now. But that bell still rings in my head. She's alive, it says. She's buying time. She's just gone fishing.

Louise Mangos

The End of the Beginning of the End

Ivan lies before us, exposed in the Arctic tundra on the hottest day of August. He is a time bomb waiting to liquefy into the ground. The permafrost that usually glues together the lichen-pocked shale has melted enough to allow the team to extract his entire body.

I take cellular samples on site, swatting away tiny mosquitoes. I'm more concerned they will alight on Ivan rather than me. As I pierce the jugular and draw a few globules of thick black blood into the syringe, I detect a movement through the air between us. I wonder if a flake of skin or an eyelash has fallen through a gap in my facemask to Ivan's cheek, binding us forever. Using fine point tweezers, I place samples of Neanderthal hair and epidermal tissue onto glass microscope plates and into doll-sized sample jars.

I help the team place his body into a plastic bag and vacuum pack it like a piece of meat being prepared for the sous-vide cooker. What little that remains of Ivan's dignity is sucked out with the air.

Before we load him into the cold truck to return to the cloning lab, I pluck a yellow marsh saxifrage from the permafrost softened by the climate change that has delivered us Ivan's body. I place it on his plastic-covered chest out of deference to his un-burial.

It is only after they've driven away that I think we should have left him to his fate. I wonder what I have just helped to unleash.

Catherine Roberts

The Road Still Glitters

It washes away – the unopened mail splashed across the kitchen table, the busted lock on the bathroom door, the whir and gurgle of Mum's nebuliser.

A breeze has the waves rippling like scalloped glass as my toes vanish in darkened sand. It is the farthest we've walked in years. Mum sits behind me on a faded towel, her prairie-green eyes meeting the seamless sea and sky.

Today, she is having a good day after a bad night.

We joined each other in the early hours as we often do, in the dips of the couch – watched a silent movie, shared a brandy until the coughing started.

"I wish I was in a traffic jam," Mum wheezed.

In these fractured nights, close to infinity, there were none of the regrets she had expected. Mum didn't wish she had made amends with friends, had more children, stuck it out with Dad, or been more charitable.

She just wanted to sit in traffic, she told me, and know that in the end, she was going somewhere.

A raptor circles overhead, the butterflied ears of a dog splash in the water. I buy a plastic spade from the stand selling dyed shells and a rainbow of sorbet, waste no time piling sand around my mother. She gathers herself up, brow pinched, but she doesn't speak.

I scoop out two seats as the sun dives, mould a steering wheel on Mum's side, four tyres, and the sweeping bonnet of a car. Smiling, Mum puts both hands on the wheel, and I climb in.

People are looking but what does that matter? What has it ever mattered? Because for now we are convinced, with the warm engine of the sand beneath us, that we could go anywhere.

That we might shatter the sea and sky.

Alison Davis

By your side

Bella's on heat. Bleeding all over your house, hormones bouncing off the ceiling. The male dogs in the neighbourhood yowl all bloody night, letting her and everyone else know they're busting their chops to get to her.

You keep her inside so you can keep an eye on her. She perches at the back door peering out, face jammed up against the glass. If you let her out, she'll roam the streets and spread her pheromones like fairy dust.

You've been through this before. One minute Lil was a playing hopscotch with scabs on her knees, and the next she was va va voom and wearing clothes that looked like underwear. Reminded you of her mum. She went out late and crawled back in smelling of no good. When you tried to talk to her, she shouted at you in a voice you didn't recognise.

And then she up and left. Just like that. Marched down the front path and out the gate with a swagger you'd only seen once before. You didn't know where she was for a while. Tidied up her room just in case she turned up one day. Last you heard, she'd skipped up north to Geraldton and shacked up with some bloke there.

You've laid some towels over a piece of foam in your bedroom so Bella will be comfortable. Vet said she'd be feeling out of sorts. You hang your arm over the edge of the bed while you're sleeping so she can nuzzle your hand during the night if she wants to. You keep her close. She's by your side for now, but you know she'll run if she gets the chance.

Ruth Moore

Housekeeping, 1937

This time, I ring the bell to make sure Mr Melville has gone before I let myself into his flat. When I drag my mop and bucket over the threshold, grey water slops onto his tiles. I shut the door, breathe, breathe. Then I start work in the living room. There are dregs of ash on the new-fangled armchairs, gin glasses smeared with lipstick. Scent hangs heavy above the gramophone. A lady was here last night, musking her territory. He treated her cordial. Surely he must, or she'd-a screamed. But me? Come and go with a mop and key - come and go in a breath. I'm something else altogether.

Yesterday, see, I came early. He was still here, lacing his shiny office shoes. He smirked, like I was a delivery. Reached towards me, laces still trailing on the floor. It was only the sound of voices in the hallway that broke the sweat-stank grip of him. I felt sick for hours after.

To the kitchen, where the coffee in the pot is all but cold. The egg has a thick layer of grease congealed atop it. I eat quickly. I eat everything, not thinking of his mouth biting into bread before mine. There's always fat pickings at Mr Melville's. Whatever he does all day at the War Office, it pays him to wastefulness.

In the bedroom, a chair lies knocked sideways. I keep working, steady, steady. I scatter salt in his sheets and crank his radiators to high heaven. I scratch his records, spit on the mirrors and tip ash into the whisky decanter. On my way out, I catch myself in the mirror, breathe, breathe.

One day soon the world will turn.

Mr Melville will be nothing but smoke.

And I will become something else altogether.

Miranda Overett

On the way to the hospital

On the way to the hospital, I stopped to go shopping. I was still pulling at my stitches with every step, still cramped around the last of my belly, but I was afraid of my uncut nails so I took slow steps past bright shelves of face creams and hair dyes, cotton wool and condom packets, to stand and contemplate scissors, clippers, nail files. I took one of everything to the checkout where a woman in a purple friendship bracelet and immaculate eyeliner did not meet my eyes, then pushed everything into the drooping pockets of my sweatpants and limped outside.

By the shiny shopfront, I ripped apart the plastic, sat down with my back against a wall and clipped away all my sharp edges, little pieces dropping to the pavement, the concrete hot beneath my legs. I ran the file across my fingertips until they were smooth and soft and pink as bubblegum, felt the sun prickle my bare shoulders, followed the averted eyes of passers by.

I stroked the file's rough edges again and again as I limped across the bright white threshold of the hospital, as I stared at the waiting room tiles, as I took my place in line to wash my hands three times under the little white tap, spray disinfectant across my wrists, pull my mask back into place and walk without counting my steps across the white, beeping room to take my place by the little corner bed with its plastic lid and its little holes, to the tiny child inside with his closed eyes who I could only touch with my fingertips, where I sat and stroked his brand new skin softly, softly, one, two, three times and again and again and again.

Elaine Gregersen

Fractured

'That's a fractured wrist.' The paediatric consultant with the beard and contained fury slices the scissors through more of my son's pyjama sleeve, exposing right forearm, elbow, shoulder, clavicle. He leans back and tuts, 'And I suspect multiple fractures.' He won't look me in the eye.

Flashback to every moment I spent with my son before rushing to hospital when I realised he wasn't using his arm. Me feeding him with a spoon. Me lifting him out of the bath. Flashback to wheeling him on to the special school bus that morning and waving as it drove away. Flashback to the hospital receptionist asking whether my five year old profoundly disabled child has a social worker and me laughing that I've begged for one for years but we all know the state of social care in this country.

'He can't tell us what happened,' I cry to a nurse. I watch her mouth my words back to a matron. I stroke my son's head and whisper 'sorry' in his ear whilst his body is x-rayed. I see the radiographer's pen noting it down.

My son lies on a table with his massacred pyjama top limp by his side. I stroke his head again. I have not done this. I don't know who has.

'No fractures!' The consultant slams the door open and yells. 'Probably just twisted it at school. Very normal for kids like yours. Weak muscles.'

We are left alone in a room with sensory toys. Hours pass and no-one comes to check on us. My son starts to use his right arm again and I record videos on my phone to show the consultant when he returns. He doesn't.

My son watches a colour-changing light. I listen to ambulances speeding towards the hospital. We wait to be remembered.

Harriet Elisabeth

A Swarm of Boys

He is running. He is running as fast as he can. He is running through the meadow and up along the stream which leads to the house. He wears a red jumper and blue shorts, his father's green Wellington boots slapping up against his knees as he runs. They are too big for him, but he insists on wearing them.

The other boys are running too; chasing him in fact. They are all dressed in the yellow shirts they are made to wear at school. They shout and jeer at him. They are like a swarm of bees, no, wasps, surging towards him.

He jumps across the stream, landing in the mud. His boots get stuck and his feet lift out. He turns around to see the boots, stumps of green stranded in the brown. His father will be angry; he isn't meant to use them, but they make him feel big.

The boys splash across the river behind him. They are a throng of yellow and noise. One of the boys picks up a boot and chucks it towards him. It stings the back of his leg.

He is nearing the house, its orange brick becoming clearer. He sees his mother through the kitchen window, she is washing up at the sink. She wears pink rubber gloves. She sees him and lifts her hand in a wave. The bubbles race down her arm.

The boys catch up to him, buzzing around in a semi-circle. Spotting the adult, one of the older boys hands him the boots he left in the mud. The boys pat him on his shoulders, smile at his mother, and turn away back down the garden.

He goes inside and falls onto the sofa. He must rest until tomorrow when it all happens again.

Fiona McKay

Falling

Britt turns five perfect cartwheels and finishes with a faultless round-off, and that's what makes her '*a natural for cheerleading*', her mom says, and if she puts down that bag of chips right now she'll keep right on fitting into her size zero cheer uniform, '*don't think I haven't noticed that little belly since Christmas*,' and Britt doesn't want this anymore – the discipline, the team, the endlessness – but her mom is so into it, like if she wants it that much let her climb pyramids of human flesh and throw herself into the abyss, or as coach calls it, '*free-somersaulting*', telling her to trust herself, trust her team-mates, trust Danny Olafson to catch her, and her mom is all '*oh Suzy Olafson and I were in school together, but she was Suzy Svenson then*,' and how '*we must get you and Danny together sometime*,' and Britt says nothing about the disco in the church basement on Halloween and Danny Olafson in that mask and what happened after, and she keeps trying to fall from the top of the pyramid but they won't let her, everyone holds her too tight, and there's no way out if she can't break out, break herself free – her mom says '*Britt, you're so clumsy these days*,' any time she sees a bruise – and she falls down the stairs, her arm held out in front of her like a sword or a shield, but even that didn't make her bleed or break, and when the nurse brings her in for the X-ray she tells Britt's mom to wait outside and says to Britt '*You need to tell us if there's any chance you might be pregnant*,' and Britt says '*No*' but maybe too fast or maybe not sure enough and now everything is falling, falling.

Malina Douglas

It's All on the Menu, Except What Fills the Ache

Sweet & Sour

Food is her medicine. Rice porridge soothes sore throats; mango offerings patch disputes. Her wok keeps food on the table; sticky rice binds the family like mortar. She raises her children on red curry and salted guava. *My hatchlings*, she calls them, spooning morsels into their mouths.

In a few thousand flicks of the spatula, her daughter is grown. Taeng packs her massaman curry for the plane. Lychee smothers the sour taste of loss.

Khao Niao Daeng

Her husband's hospital bills are rising. She checks his insulin. Khao niao daeng would not be red without palm sugar. She sweetens with monk fruit and colours with beetroot. Recoils. The dish is blood-bright.

Expenses rise and Taeng cooks faster. She wipes sweat from her bow. She has no time for the sensation like chillies burning under her skin. Sweetens cakes with bananas and they fly off the shelves.

Slow down, says her husband. She ignores him.

Som Tam

The wok belches flame as Taeng cooks. The queue is out the door. She sways on her feet.

A tourist complains her som tam is too spicy, but she put only one chilli. She prefers four. Burns off regrets till her eyes water.

Bad reviews sink her mood and her customers slow to a trickle.

Perhaps food cannot fix everything, but it *has* to. She throws herself into gluten free brownies and keto cakes. Her daughter refuses to visit. Gorges till sugar-sick.

She's baking lava cake while stirring a pot of curry when she collapses.

Tom Yum Soup

Taeng wakes to the smell of tom yum and her husband's worried eyes. Has he stirred the curry, checked the oven? The symphony of keffir lime and galangal soothes her senses. A steaming spoon veers towards her and she opens her mouth.

Tim Craig

A Question of Questions

The accident investigator sees a lot of things.

This is what he tells his wife at dinner: 'I see a lot of things, you know?'

'Yes,' says his wife.

He waves his spoon for emphasis.

'Things you would not want to see.'

'I am sure of it.'

The accident investigator slurps at the winter soup like a man who has seen many things. A bead of carrot in his moustache dances as he speaks.

'More than anything else, it is a question of questions,' he says.

He rearranges the glasses and cutlery on the table to demonstrate.

'Who was driving too fast here? Who missed the STOP sign? Who braked too late?'

They sit and contemplate the objects on the tablecloth in silence.

It is the kind of silence which might once have been interrupted by the telephone: their daughter calling from Prague.

The next day, as usual, the accident investigator sees a lot of things.

Driving home, he nearly hits a deer on an unlit forest road; it is a reminder that, for all they have seen, accident investigators are not themselves immune from accidents.

Arriving back late, he finds the house dark, the kitchen table bare, and no winter soup on the stove.

He calls his wife's name, but there is no answer.

The accident investigator walks around the kitchen, examining the scene from all possible angles.

'Who is to blame here?' he says.

'Who was not paying attention? Who is at fault?'

Damhnait Monaghan

Baby Blues

"She's gorgeous."

The woman at the table next to you stretches to stroke Charlotte's cheek. Her diamond ring dazzles in the sunlight stealing in through the café window. You recognise the maternal yearning, the desperate ache. But you aren't sharing. You pull Charlotte closer, burying your nose in her dark curls, inhaling the apricot scent of baby shampoo. You love her fiercely; you could bite her feather soft cheeks. But you kiss them, left, then right, claiming her, like an explorer planting a flag.

"She has your eyes."

The woman at the table next to you won't shut up. But you don't correct her, don't say Charlotte doesn't have your eyes, could never have your eyes. You don't explain the science: that eyes are like snowflakes, no two are identical, not even on the same face. You don't chide the woman, don't tell her if she opened her own eyes and looked closely, she'd see that your eyes are a steely blue, while Charlotte's are the soft grey of a mourning dove.

"She does, right?"

The woman at the table next to you insists upon a response. But you don't give her one. You don't tell her that if she paid attention, really paid attention, she'd see that the irises in Charlotte's eyes are speckled, like eggs. Like the eggs your body refuses to hatch. You don't reveal that sometime soon, if your sister-in-law doesn't watch her little chick more closely, you and Charlotte are going to fly.

"Bye, bye."

Alison Woodhouse

Flying high melted more than the beeswax in his wings

Cecelia lies on a lounger, on the terrace of her first husband's house, her home for a while.

Blaise had waved her in without comment. After a necessary shower she'd dressed in borrowed linen shirt and boxer shorts because her own clothes were marred by travel. They'd sipped thimblefuls of black coffee and navigated a conversation around her impending divorce from husband number three, Blaise unable to hide his satisfaction. When she said she needed rest, he'd ushered her outside.

She zones in on the lapping of the river against the wall less than a metre away, insects droning around the purple spikes of lavender that she'd planted all those years ago, the midday chimes from the church up the hill. She sheds clothes, stretches her body.

'Would you like an parasol?' Blaise is an outline under the pergola, which has weathered to a silver grey. Cecelia reaches for her shirt. 'No need,' he says.

'Alright. I haven't felt such glorious heat for so long.'

'These days I think it's wiser to avoid the sun. Once burnt, you know.'

'Really?'

She hears the plop of a cast, pictures the flick of a fin as a carp darts towards the bait, a fisherman on the opposite bank in sturdy boots, legs wide, thighs braced, a rod bending, quivering, water foaming, the fish thrashing, red oozing from the gash in its gill, fighting, fighting, before slipping the hook, darting into the reeds, hiding in the murky gloom.

Cecelia rises, climbs up on the wall, balances with arms above her head. Dark green fronds ripple below, like grass in a breeze. Blaise shouts out.

The water is shockingly cold, but only for a moment, then it is silky like a wedding gown.

Donna L. Greenwood

Brown Dog

She's been stannin' for so long, she's womb-sore. Her fifth came away from her three days ago – little more than froth and blood. She cleyned it away from her thighs with rough wool and ash. Two of her own are on trial with her today. The eldest girl's right goffy – should have dreawned her when she was a babby. And the boy's allus fratching over some'at.

The Dul's here awlreet. In the sweat of the steaming crowd. In the owd man in front of her. Flickering black tongue. Accusing her of things he wishes he could do. His skin stinks of piss and ale.

She's for a hanging. She sees it on the faces of her kin. Their hatred is a gut punch. It leaves her wheezing. Never could keep a man. Too hard. Too mean. Lone woman. Birthing childer with no fayther. A witch awlreet.

She kiddied her youngest that she had a brown devil dog called Ball that'd kill whoever she asked it to. The child was feart and that made her glad. Eased her own hurting somehow. But now she's moithered. There's squirming in her stomach. She remembers the other things she told her youngest. Not true. Just for a laugh. To watch the child skrike and go all yawpish.

The crowd is quietening. Jennet, nine-years-old, is pushed forward by smiling men. She's skenning at her. Embers for eyes. There's cruelty in the twist of her gob. She's her mam's daughter awlreet.

Anika Carpenter

In Response to the Fifth Rent Hike

I ripped up the carpets. Replaced them with twenty tons of soil. Planted oak saplings and sycamores in the living room. Atlas cedars, aspens and hornbeams in the bedroom. I introduced badgers, woodpeckers, and tawny owls. Left a message on my landlord's phone:

I am no longer your tenant. I am a groundskeeper and expect to be paid accordingly.

My landlord appeared unannounced. Found the front door wedged open by fountain grass, and me, standing on the stone steps, enjoying a thin cigar, its smoke curling into the shape of a beckoning hand. All scowls, tight-shouldered he followed me in, past the ivy-covered coat rack and walls laced with snails' incomprehensible journeys. He cursed at what had once been a tiled hallway, but was now a muddy path. I showed off the kitchen first.

Fungi flourished under the breakfast table, old man's beard made a soft cloud of the pan rail, fallen leaves softened the floor. 'I'd offer you a tea' I said, 'but a nuthatch is nesting in the kettle.' My landlord's cheeks flushed red as fly agaric. "Tell me the whole place isn't like this.'

Upstairs squirrels skittered across curtain rails. Branches tickled cornices. Shy curls of ferns echoed patterns in wallpaper that had become foggy, indistinct. Like something emerging from a mist. My landlord grabbed me by the collar, raged, 'I'll fill skips with felled trees and withered plants. I'll have every animal stuffed!' He was answered by bramble roots breaking through the ceiling, dislodged earthworms landing writhing in his hair, a mouse-sized bat swooping from the rafters to claim a place in the lining of his suit jacket. 'You do understand,' I said, eyeing his clenched fists, 'pipistrelles are protected by law. To injure that creature, to disturb its home, that would be a criminal act.'

Anne Falkowski

Scavengers

"I'm sick of them shitting everywhere." The old lady yells at Walter.

We seagulls form a line on the couple's roof. Wind whips. Waves swell. The ocean nearby. We perch on the roof of their trailer each day at noon even though the old lady recently paid some guy to put metal spikes up.

She yells because Walter forgot his hearing aids. She pops a beer. Holds it out. Walter doesn't take it. She sets it on the table, next to the paper plate holding his hotdog.

Everyone's eyeing the hotdog.

"Pay attention." I shout to my easily distracted crew. "We are here to show her who's boss!"

We are also here for the view. Toddlers drop donuts. Teenagers abandon French Fries. Crabs crawl out of low tide. We hear the song of blues when blues are running. From this place, we are Gods. She's a fool to think metal spikes will keep us away. Walter used to whistle Broadway tunes while casting his line when the blues ran. Now he sits in a lawn chair. Oxygen tube up each nostril.

The gull with one leg lands last. "What did I miss? Did we shit on her deck yet?"

Just as I'm about to say you haven't missed much, the clamor of sirens tears through the salt air. An ambulance brakes in front of the trailer. We hold ourselves steady. Pipe ourselves down. Out comes a stretcher and two EMT's who rush towards Walter.

We seagulls fly off. It's the right thing to do. Give them privacy. We call out to each other. We soar over ocean. Foamy waves buckle at high tide. "We'll be back." Our voices churn in unison, knowing we will be there tomorrow, whether she throws away the hotdog or not.

Lisa Thornton

They Say There Are No Questions Asked

Somewhere in a canyon, a man with a folding table gives out hearts for the heartbroken. Colorful ones stitched by his grandmother. Plastic painted ones. Ceramic ones and ones made from old bee hives.

The line sometimes snakes all the way into town. The reds, oranges, yellows and blues of people's vests and hats fill the crevice in the earth like a flash flood rainbow.

They say the man is related to the tamale lady with her shouts and her basket. They say he is from Mexico and Chile and Argentina.

He folds up his table at the first sign of storms. The lucky ones brag back in the bars. They puff their chests and lean onto jukeboxes, looking for love to visit them again.

They say his hearts are the best hearts. The kind that weigh as much as a dozen eggs, that don't stop working in the heat of summer when the sun begins to set marking quitting time or when a baby crying in the next room suddenly goes silent or when your beloved says they are sorry, it's not like them, really. That's not who they are. It's just been so hard lately. Not even when a fist pounds a tabletop demanding forgiveness, coffee cups and saucers clinking, shaking, shaking there on the table until there is no more life in them, and they stop moving.

They say his hearts are homemade. They say they last forever.

Joanna Miller

Belonging

Philomena forages the foreshore, collecting heart-shaped cockles and sea lettuce, a lone solid figure silhouetted against the gunmetal grey of the horizon. Before the breakfast crowds arrive, she heads back along the main street, pitching from side to side like a coble in a rough sea, passing the pretty fishermen's cottages with their sandbags stacked high against the front doors, to her own, all peeling paint, cobweb-laced windows, and unsightly tufts of dead grass in the gutter.

Although the new neighbours call her a character, Philomena knows their talk is unkind, that they complain when her cats yowl at night, and look away when she sits on the balcony eating winkles with a pin. Even the house is reproachful; *Cornelius would never have let things get to this state*, it says. But it's been over five years since Cornelius took his last earthly breath.

Philomena is mindful of all this and wonders when she became the outsider. She picks up one of the retirement home brochures her daughter sent, turns the glossy pages, and tries to imagine living there. Yes, she could take some of her things - the old clock, his chair, the photos - and yet, a lifetime of hopes, tears, and laughter are woven into the fabric of this house.

He's calling out to her now in that soft Irish voice, "You won't leave me here, will you Philomena?"

She shakes her head, "I will not."

She knows she is of this place, at one with the moon and the tides. When the storm makes landfall, when the winter wind roars and the waves crash against the sea wall reaching as far up as The Bistro, while the incomers tremble, she steps out into the night, her coat billowing behind her, like a galleon setting sail.

Pedro Ponce

Orson Welles

Be prepared, admonished the evening news. *Know the signs*. Shoes scuffled urgently on the pavement below. Dogs up and down the block howled into the purpling sky.

Close enough, I thought. I opened the emergency kit.

The case folded out into a shelter for one. Stenciled inside were instructions for determining the most deserving member in your group. I could afford to ignore these as I sifted through the packets spilling onto the basement floor.

There was a first-aid kit and a deck of cards. The cards were smaller than the usual deck and backed with green camouflage. There were dry rations and rations that could be activated with potable water, seven days each. I nibbled on the miniature chocolates in the pop-up plastic jack-o'-lantern. I assembled the Christmas tree and put a Fourth of July sparkler where the star should be. I started the needlepoint commemorating national history. My stitches grew clumsy in the glare of the spent sparkler. The rampant eagle rising in the east seemed to yawn in its inevitable trajectory to the west.

The purple outside had turned to black. I put batteries into the emergency torch and rolled it next to the Christmas tree. For my safety, and to preserve battery life, the light was only as bright as Orson Welles' cigar as he narrated the latest. The water heater and washing machine grew solid in the dim orange glow. Pages of newsprint piled on the floor, wrinkled dramatically and dusted with ash. The National Guard had been summoned. The President would address the nation at any moment. A bow tie hung from the clothesline overhead. Orson Welles sipped from a steel tumbler. The ice in his drink chimed, amplified by the ziggurat of his microphone. It was almost time to play solitaire.

Shelley Roche-Jacques

Coco Chunnel

Dad's buggered off down the Anchor for a Boxing Day pint, leaving Mum to entertain his two sisters. Chrissy and Jacky went to grammar school and came out speaking like they have plums in their mouths, but Mum still wants them to like her. She's using the best tablecloth, is getting the Babycham glasses out to make Snowballs, and there's a big sherry trifle for later. They're asking what Dad got her for Christmas and she's acting all coy, so I pipe up and tell them he got her some really posh perfume. They say 'ooh' and 'how marvellous' and primp their big stiff hair helmets. Mum just smiles and runs her finger round the holly embroidered on the tablecloth, so I run upstairs to get the bottle.

'In celebration of the commencement of the new Channel Tunnel project,' I tell them, reading from the box. 'It's like *Coco Chanel*,' I add, holding the big rectangular bottle up close to their faces so they can get a proper look. 'Limited edition. Fresh notes of the white cliffs of Dover carefully blended with the hot, doughy undertones of a Parisian bakery.' This makes them whoop and tell Mum what an 'awfully lucky girl' she is.

When they've gone Mum tells me to go and put the bottle back in her room. When I come back down, she's sitting at the kitchen table shovelling great spoonfuls of the massive trifle into her mouth straight from the serving bowl.

Alison Powell

No Room for Love

It's 2am and I know, from the smell of cigarettes, that Marlon Brando is in my living room again. Not *The Godfather* Brando, with his jutting chin, but the 1951 *Streetcar* vintage complete with Kowalksi's muscle-tight t-shirt and disdain.

There was a time when his appearance would have caused me to slip into a negligee. To slink around the doorway, eyeing him through the smoke. To ask if he thought it possible that I was once considered — attractive?

These days I know better.

I slump out of bed in fleece pyjamas, head down to make cocoa, barely bother to glance at Brando's pouting lips.

He's at his best – they all are: Matt Dillon in the kitchen wearing that *Rumble Fish* white vest, the sweat still fresh on his skin like he's just back from the fight. Al Pacino soaking in the bathtub drinking his *Scarface* champagne, calling me 'doll' despite the talks we've had. De Niro spinning that gun in the hallway mirror. And out on the porch, Newman and Redford lean against the doorframe, their *Sundance* hands on their hips.

I've asked them all to leave. Time and again I've said: 'This can't go on. How can I bring someone home with you lot filling the space?'

But the men won't go.

My sister said I should move house, which worked at first – I've had a few quiet weeks: three dreary dates, a sordid fuck in a club.

Then yesterday I awoke to the sound of the bathtub filling, the flicking of the gun, the smell of smoke.

'We've had this date with each other from the beginning!' drawls Brando now.

'You talkin' to me?' says de Niro.

'Who do I trust?' says Pacino. 'Me! That's who.'

All of them are back.

And in a way, I am relieved.

Gemma Church

A not-so super position

My dead husband's voice wakes me. I'm not surprised. He wakes me every morning.

He asks: "Would you like to know what the weather will be like today?"

I say: "No."

"Do you want me to play some music? If so, what genre or artist?"

"No."

"Shall I open the curtains? It's lovely outside and - "

"NO!"

He pulls the curtains open anyway. I bury my head under the duvet, which smells like wet dog now even though we don't have a dog. It's better than facing the light that's laser-beaming in through the bedroom window.

I move the covers so only my mouth pokes out. A scene from *Red Dwarf* flashes through my head. Vindoloovians? If Jeff was here, he'd draw an eyeball on my chin and laugh.

Instead, I yell: "Can you suffocate and die under a duvet?"

I cross my fingers.

There's a pause.

I wonder if his algorithms are reconfiguring, trying to work out the best response.

"Are you having a medical episode? Your breathing and heart rates appear within the normal parameters, according to your smartwatch. But shall I make a pre-emptive call to a medical professional?"

I return to my duvet cocoon.

No one can see me under here, trapped in a superposition between death and life. Like that fucking cat in a box. I forget the scientist's name. Schwimmer? Schumacher? Schulz?

Jeff would have known. He was a scientist. He worked away in the desert on super-sensitive experiments. No one was allowed a phone. I set the so-called smart speaker to use his voice while he was away. To feel less lonely.

Now, I'm lonelier than ever. But I can't turn him off.

And I can't stand having him simultaneously both here and not here either.

It's killing me.

Sherryl Clark

I have never drowned, not literally

My brother likes to tell the story of when he drowned. At the last moment, our sister reached down into the creek and grabbed his long, curly, blond locks and hauled him out. Of course it was heroic. But then they had to tell Mum.

I can only imagine what she said, how our sister would have been scolded for letting him play down there in the first place, how he would have been scolded for being so stupid, and then 'just wait until your father hears about it'. Maybe he would have received a cuddle and perhaps a kiss after all that.

Who knows? My brother only remembers the rescue, and my sister is dead now.

I have never rescued anyone, not literally. No running into burning buildings, no swimming out past the breakers to haul a half-dead person to shore, not even a resuscitation effort.

My pets died by accident or of old age. My house plants sagged and withered when they decided they'd had enough.

And now here we all are, upside down in a bus at the bottom of a ravine, and I already know that it's too late for some of us. Perhaps it's too late for me as well. I can't feel anything, and that may not be a good sign. The blood dripping down my shirt is not mine, at least. I can hear moaning, and someone shouting 'Oh God, oh God' over and over. I want to crawl out and finally rescue someone, even if it is only myself, but I can't move.

All I can do is lie here and wait, and picture my brother's curls floating and that strong, sure hand reaching down and lifting him up.

Rebekah Clarkson

Best Day Ever

I was feeling grateful and also bad because my sister had abruptly left work after I'd choked down the phone that my husband's GP had rung to say that he was concerned for my husband's safety and would not let him drive home alone but would send him to hospital in an ambulance, which my husband had begged him not to do, unless I was able to pick him up, which of course I wasn't, because our only car was now at the doctor's surgery. I had found my husband alone in a room with the door not closed but also not open. My sister gave me a wink from the waiting area as my husband and I went back into the GP's room where he talked in circles until I also agreed that the mental health care system was indeed broken. My sister then drove my husband back to her house while I went and found us all lunch from a nearby café, thinking and thinking about what I should do next. The three of us sat in the sun in my sister's backyard eating organic salads with the last of the stumps of a tree that had fallen over in last year's storm and had made my sister cry wondering how much longer it had lived there before us. I was still thinking about what to do next when I turned to my sister and said thank you so much for helping us, for just leaving work, for dropping everything. My sister looked at me with the pursed smile that is distinctively hers, and then looked at my husband, cocked an eyebrow and said, '*Best day ever*,' and this remains one of the funniest and kindest things anyone has ever said to me.

Fiona Lynch

Subcutaneous

A boy in a black hoodie; an orange-tipped hypodermic.

A boy with a haversack skates to meet friends; spare needles buckled in khaki.

A boy coached to refuse sweets learns to triple flip; on a good day, 80mg into a thigh holds him.

A boy drops frontside spins, nollie heel flips—others at the skate park can't match him; school camp, classmates find his kit, pretend to collapse yelling, 'Get me jelly babies, get me jelly babies,' and he laughs until they leave the cabin.

A boy turns 15, tired of hypos, of being called A Big Jelly Baby; a new kid with a backwards cap doesn't know, calls him behind a bush, his own spoon and needle.

A boy under plumbago is not breathing; the spoon kid slides the needle out, scarpers.

A boy is found, pulse thin as cotton; an ambulance officer narcans his nostrils, one, two, three, four times.

A boy battles to see 16; ventilated, almost everything he needs through an IV, respite from needles.

A boy who only wanted camouflage headlines the newsfeed; a politician lures media to a hospital carpark, 'The drug war will only get worse with safe injecting houses.'

A boy's sleeping forehead kissed by dad, mum stroking his arm, 'Everything'll be ok love'; the politician knifes and needles—the family, law enforcement, gutless government. Leaving the foyer, a Channel 9 mike caws for comment. Chin to chest, dad mumbles, 'We're a family, not a story. Leave us alone. And that mouthy pollie, he's just a prick trying to score points.'

A boy breathes in, and breathes out, tubing looped through fresh pyjamas; meds syringed into a port, the insertion site collared, iodine tides his dressings. Clear adhesive protects the skin where saline sustains him. And bedside, every morning, hungry, colourless tears.

Jeanette Lowe

Coffee cup

She settles across the train aisle and I breathe in her sweet citrus scent. Take a look. Pale pink polo, chunky gold chain.

I haven't worn perfume in months. Years, probably.

There's a takeaway cup wedged behind the right bum cheek of her skin-tight jeans. On its side, plastic lid firm, mud-coloured liquid dripping to the floor. She hasn't noticed. Doesn't seem to feel it.

She slips her laptop out of her leather rucksack. Starts tapping at the keyboard. Checks her phone, taps some more. I keep quiet. A struggle. You're squidging a cup and making the already mucky carpet stickier, more disgusting. What about those little kids, shoes off, padding along the aisle? How come you don't care?

One of the children stops. Leans against the seat in front, looks at her, looks at me, pads back down the carriage.

And what kind of person would leave half a coffee on a seat? What's wrong with the table, or taking it with you? What's wrong with finishing it?

I'm too old to be a mother now. It isn't her fault, it isn't the coffee-leaver's fault. It isn't your fault for quitting after the baby died. People do what they want. What they can.

The train slows. She closes the laptop and slides it into her rucksack. When she gets up the cup tumbles to the floor. She doesn't so much as glance at it.

Her face floats past my window, chin up, eyes forward. I pick up the cup and hold it on my flip-down table, fingers clamped. When the train eases forward the *Any rubbish please* person with the see-through sack enters the carriage. I keep tight-hold. Perhaps something warm and soothing will leach into my bloodstream. Something strong enough to thaw me.

Heather D Haigh

Smelly Dog You Need a Clean, Filthy Bitch Your Teeth are Green

Clap-clap

There'll be a day when Anna holds a party by flickering candlelight, with voodoo masks, needle-stuck dolls, the scent of cheap vodka, and the urgent need to have her lipstick smeared.

Today is not that day.

Today, Anna squinches at Dad's snores and air gulps her churning belly to a quiet nausea. A sooted candle stump, wax clumping upon the chipped saucer, sputters out.

The cooker won't work.

The shilling jar's empty.

Yesterday, Anna helped herself to bread and marg with sugar. Today the bread's grown green hair, and the marg wrapper cringes beside an overflowing bin. Colonies of slumping crystals lurk in tacky brown pools on the worktops. Six plates, one pan, nine brown-ringed mugs, and eleven cloudy glasses jostle in a sink full of drain-stinky water, blobbed with lardy grease turds. The tap is dripping.

The mank makes her eyes prickle. Not because Katrina's kitchen has shiny taps and a floor that isn't sticky—and this Anna knows because Katrina's mum put a plaster on Anna's knee last week and wiped away her snot, blood and tears, with no mean words or slaps. And not because, at home-time, as Anna slipped between the adults, Johnny's mum said *soap and water* in a whisper everyone could hear.

But because—this morning—Dad promised he would clean the kitchen. That he would bring out the tablecloth from the sideboard, the tablecloth that used to smell of soapy lemons and the whoosh of a hot iron, and the garden in summer. And of mum. But now it smells of socks and old mushrooms and is covered in black bruises.

But mostly because—today, all day, Anna's been daydreaming, never daring to hope, but daydreaming all the same, of pink icing and eight white candles.

Barbara Diggs

Hope Is A Four-Letter Word

You take the weak beam of sunlight struggling through the green-grey skies as an omen: today, you will approach her. You know the experts say it's hopelesss. But you also know that, as a mother, you're doomed to be burdened with hope.

Packs of the infected have swarmed your neighborhood, lurching past your window for over a year now. You've learned to filter out the waxy, rotting skin, the rusty filth of their clothes, the sunken eyes, the deep hungering moans. You only watch for the goddess braids she'd started wearing before her infection, candy-apple red locks dangling to her waist. You see her daily, or the girl that was her, braids stringy and matted, shuffling down the same sidewalk where she learned to skateboard; the same sidewalk where you waited, braced, for her to barrel into your open arms.

You see him as well, the one who infected her, stumbling alongside her, his tattered Straight Outta T-shirt clinging improbably to his decaying remains. It occurs to you that, in the end, you were both right about him. Last week, you saw the pair of them in your yard, tearing into a blood-glistened torso right where your pink azaleas used to be. When a small pack shambled over, her infector swung a humerus at them, over and over, allowing her to feed undisturbed. Experts say the infected do not love, but you know what you saw. You fell back from the window, sickening gratitude twisting your heart.

You've long resisted the temptation of dubious powders and pills, pricey treatment programs, silver-tongued charlatans. But today, when she ambles past, you'll hurry to stand before her on the pavement, arms spread wide. Hoping, yes, but braced for whatever comes next, even the feel of her teeth sinking into your flesh.

S.A. Greene

After The Last Man on Earth Switches off His Alarm Clock

he wonders why the bedroom's so bloody cold. Then he remembers. He pulls on the white cashmere dressing-gown he got one Christmas from the late Last Woman on Earth.

But then it gets too bloody hot. The Last Man on Earth looks for his Speedos, then laughs in a *what-am-I-like?* kind of way when he remembers.

He swims, naked and serene, along Whitehall, proud that everything he sees belongs to him now, even Nelson's Column, poking up above the surface of the water like that.

After a lovely supper of tinned salmon and crackers, The Last Man on Earth waves to The Man in The Moon.

'Good evening, my friend!' he shouts through the dining-room window.

The Man in The Moon doesn't reply.

The Last Man on Earth opens a new bottle of old wine. He strokes his Rolex and the hairs on his wrist, and then his forearm. He waves at the Man in the Moon again, but the Man in the Moon still doesn't take any notice. The Last Man on Earth downs more wine. Perhaps The Man in The Moon didn't hear him from the dining-room. That must be it. D'oh! He opens the bi-fold doors and staggers outside onto the immaculate plastic lawn.

It's raining again. Hard. And the wind! *Oh God, this fucking wind!*

And The Last Man on Earth falls to his knees, lifts his soaking face to the skies, and begs The Man in The Moon to wave back to him.

Dawn Miller

No One Can Figure Out How Eels Have Sex

They navigate through the Sargasso Sea, an army of eels marching on their stomachs. We imagine them slithering around aquatic forests like how we skirt the reedy boys on the playground, sparse hairs sprouting above their lips, soft as a girl's.

The boys snap our bra straps when teachers aren't looking. Shoot spitballs the grown-ups say equal love. Maleness hurricanes our armor, slippery and newborn. We learn: a girl is an eel is a mystery is a target.

Stories swirl at recess. Is that the woman they found in the garbage dump? Or the athlete burnt alive? The one in the department store dressing room? On the bus? The train? The cruise ship?

We gather, our minds brimming with news flashes and parental warnings: a girl is an eel is a chameleon is a statistic.

Sex organs aren't visible in a dissected eel, the books say, scientists scratching their heads. But eels know the mysteries of their own bodies. We layer sweatshirts over T-shirts to hide our nipples, bind our legs with thick tights, stay home from school when the bleeding flows the worst. We learn to punch with our knuckles, carry house keys in our fists, practice how to kick so it hurts the most.

Anguilla, we call our eel selves, like warriors, and spit out doom scrolls and sex education half-truths. We brace ourselves under a glass-like surface, heavy as the sea, while we watch for predators and the next bad thing that'll most surely come.

Tim Boiteau

Like It or Not

Evelyn logged seven hours and thirty-one minutes of sleep. One like.

Ten-minute pre-breakfast yoga. Two likes.

Image of one latte, bowl of fat blueberries, and cup of vanilla Yoplait. One like.

Another latte, which she almost sipped before snapping a pic and posting online. No likes. But still, the principle of the matter.

Thumbed through a bit of Rumi while taking a shit, and tweeted an excerpt, something about thoughts becoming birds, a vague deadnaming of Twitter, though she didn't ruminate on this long enough to fully grasp the meaning. Eleven likes.

She logged her two-mile commute by bicycle to the office. Four likes.

The morning, between snatches of tedium, consisted of Office and cat memes, all garnering a total of twelve likes.

At lunch her phone swallowed a salmon salad, and she admired the image while barely glancing at the flaky meat passing her lips via fork. Twenty likes. Damn-good photo.

More afternoon memes of Michael Scott and Darth Vader and Emily in Paris and a photo of another latte plagiarized from online, as Evelyn forgot to photograph the one she actually drank after her 1500-step-count trip to Starbucks. Likage accumulation of thirty one, many from her mom and a cousin recuperating from ankle surgery.

Cocktails after work—fotographia de muchas sangrias y tapas. Trece likes. Or is it me gustas?

Drunk-cycling home with typo-filled post. Zero likes.

Leftovers, unappealing visually and in every other sense. No post. No likes. This riddled her with more guilt than she could explain. But as an act of contrition she entered her phone and liked every single one of the posts her friends, family, acquaintances, and strangers had left since her end-of-day doomscroll yesterday evening.

Which is also how she spent the rest of the evening.

Rachael Smart

Four for a Boy

When you do the taking, stocky men will accompany you. They will look solemn as magpies in their black and white uniforms, beaks firmly closed, radios fizzing static. You must focus on threshold criteria and harm ratios on the business and stride down, with the empty car seat hefty in your hands, or you might turn back, you might leave.

In a crack-white side room, you will try hard to shrink the image of a mother clutching to her baby and your knowledge of the passage to come. Is *[insert applicable name]* ready for us now. It is not a question.

Most babies look alike with their startled cloudy eyes, the hard rack of pink gums. Some mew in your arms with powdery skin still pickled from their mother's warm sac.

There will be one young woman who vixens around in front of you, on haunches, with saliva strings slick between sprung jaws, and another who knees you hard, swiftly, in the thigh, the pain of which won't hurt nearly enough. One will shriek you cannot do this whilst she witnesses you doing it. There will be one who asks – so courteously – if she can have just another hour as though she ,may be asking amicably for a little more sleep, a tepid bottle, cellular blanket, toast.

On the way out, the baby will be harnessed inside the car seat, blown glass delicate, a cosmic weight in your hands. The mother's rapacious screech from the room you left her in will spook the blue blood of you and there will be a rising siren from the one taken.

You will have to lean on a railing, a door, anything solid, to catch your breath and one of the men will say: Come on now, love, we've just got to keep moving.

Allison Field Bell

Living Room

They can't find the cat. There are no stars, and there is no moon. That's the smoke. They smell it. Like a campfire only thicker and heavier and full of something else. Fear. Or maybe that's just them: their bodies. Moving through the house. They can't find the cat. The daughter is made distraught by this, small lips trembling. Pickles, she calls out the backdoor. Nothing. Only stillness. The mother scolds her. The daughter says: Pickles is my best friend. As if that were relevant. As if the mother were somehow to blame. As if the new glow on the horizon didn't look like death. As if the car wasn't already waiting for them in the driveway. The husband honking. The son sobbing silently. Let's go, the mother says. Pickles will be okay. The daughter refuses. Pickles will be dead. The husband honks. They don't have time for this. The glow is stronger. An orange line. Like the world is cracking in half there. And maybe it is. The mother grabs the daughter who screams and kicks with all her small might. The mother hauls her through the house, the living room. The living room: a room for the living. In the car now: all of them. The husband drives fast. No one on their street. Every house dark and empty. Orange glow at their heels. No sirens. No car horns or calls for the cat. Only the orange. Only one way forward, one way out. The cat no longer matters. Just the car and their lives contained within it. The living room. Their hearts beat in unison. The father presses the gas pedal harder. The mother grips her seatbelt. The son whimpers. The daughter cries. But there they are: alive and living, and behind them, the world turns orange.

Christy Hartman

Try Again, Again

Yesterday my sister stopped by under the guise of cheering me up. Without pausing for breath, she dug her nails into my pain, borrowing crumbs of my grief to fuel her stagnant afternoon. Her greedy baby giggled and cooed, angling for a piece of my shredded heart.

I avoided indulgent questions by massaging her maternal ego. "You must be tired. He's a sweet boy." If I'd prayed to the God I don't believe in, would I be the one lamenting chafed nipples and thinning hair?

Today I'm back at work, robotically expressing gratitude for the three days they allotted my grief. One day for my baby's butterfly-winged heartbeat to slow and stop; for her porcelain body to be ripped from mine in a flurry of sterile instruments and blood. One day to wilt in bed, the ghost of my daughter nestled at my breast, whispering the name I'd only shared with her. One day to erect a fortress around my anguish, to keep it from eliciting awkward apologies and uncomfortable stares. No one acknowledges the dead baby in the room. I'm thankful. Devastated. Infuriated.

Tonight, my husband tiptoes carefully; everything he says is wrong. I'm sorry (for what?), I understand (you don't), I want to help (you can't). His grief is valid. Mine is inescapable, tattooed across my doughy stomach, an initiation to a sisterhood I'm no longer part of. Tonight, I blame him, myself, the doctors, and the God who doesn't listen.

Tomorrow I will try again, again.

Sally Khan

Henry Hilltops

Henry lived in the attic. An old soldier who wailed through toothless black gums and a coarse white beard, high on end-of-life treats. Almost every night. During the day he would hunker by his stove, burn milk and ready himself for whatever was to come. Much like he had done in his foxhole. But sometimes, in what must have been a frenzy of impotent rage, he would throw off his blankets and wreck his room. His bare, sticky feet squealing on the cratered Lino as he dragged his bed and chair. Shuddering out a rhythm as if lost in delirious dance. But he wasn't dancing, or wrecking. He was chasing mice. He knew he had no chance of ever catching the rapid little fuckers, but if he could do enough to frighten them - then perhaps they would think twice the next time the stench of unwashed plates drove them mad enough to join his party.

And when the nights at *Hilltops* became peaceful - with no wailing or dancing - everyone on the Wednesday morning *Stretch & Meditate* class in the community room figured Henry was working through a stay at St Mary's. And they wished him well. And then swapped tips on Melatonin and Valerian.

It wasn't until their sleep became ambushed by an intensive, scratching scuttle and the smell of cadaverine, that a call was made to the warden. Who called management. Who called the exterminator, who held his nose against the sweet, putrid stench and opened the door to Henry's cathedral. To an avalanche of tadpole-rodents. Churning his occupancy in a cadaverous blur, a beautifully choreographed jiggle of unprocessed trauma and trashed credit. Now just another stain on the mattress that the cleaner would have to get help from the handyman. To flip over.

Simon Cowdroy

6pm. Your BP is 190 over 110, and you are driving 15mph over the speed limit….

….Do you wish me to send a medical alert, Angela?

No, I sodding don't, what I want is a smartwatch that doesn't nag when I'm snoring like a hibernating bear circling the drain of sleep apnoea after a quart of Shiraz, or my blood pressure has attained 'she's gunna blow, Captain' status, but concentrates instead on normal watch stuff, like a bloody alarm to tell me that for the third time in a fortnight I'm late to pick up Cassidy, and yes, I did accidentally set it to silent mode, but what is the fuckity fucking point of this AI bullshit if it can't work out when I've cocked up, and anyway Nathan's to blame for buying me the damn thing, and it's his fault I'm doing the school run after work because he's decided for us he needs a career break to centre his chakra, which is a laugh because he can't centre a piss into a bowl from two feet, and tonight he's atop Mount Centennial cocooned in turquoise silk protesting with 'kindred spirits' from Sleeping Bags for Somalia (Registered Charity), and here's hoping an earth tremor sends them barrelling downhill like corpulent glowworms, especially that Theresa Kennedy who gawps at Nathan like he's first prize in the meat raffle, and shit, I lose it on that corner and hit the horn, but the roadside crowd just smiles beatifically before eventually scattering, which seems strange until I spy the Honk for Equality banners, and I'm a good person so stick a supportive thumb out the window, but all I get back are middle fingers as I've demolished their Waffles for Intersectionality stand before course-correcting, and I'm still five miles from Cassidy and Miss Frigging Watson who will be mumbling something about Child Services.

Finnian Burnett

Mannequin Body Parts

Alfred, that's the man's name. He cleans up after the others go, green coverall zipped to the neck, push broom making a slow, steady path.

Hi Betty, he says to an arm twisted over the edge of a mail cart. *Shelley*, he calls to plastic legs behind piled cardboard boxes.

Alfred talks about his day, how his wife came through cataract surgery, *thank you Lord*, and how his grandchild learned to say Pappy.

Raylene, he says, lifting a torso from the cold tile floor. He places it on the shelf next to a redhead with crimson lips. *Sit here next to Barbara.*

We don't know how he knows our names when we don't know them ourselves, but we believe him. One plastic pile of parts becomes Norma, another Jennifer

Oh Martha, Alfred says, his voice deep with emotion. *What have they done?* His hands cradle detached fingers, sort them into proper order. *They don't mean* it, he says.

Alfred eases a headless body back into a shelf. He lumbers around the room, looking for the head. A stock boy kicked it under a shelf earlier and it's buried in the dust now, staring for eternity at moldy baseboards. *I'm sorry, Candice*, he says, covering her headless body with a cloth.

We stare at the walls, the ceiling—wherever they've thrown us, wherever our gazes have landed. Our sprawled collection of breasts, limbs, and necks breathe in silence for Candice, secretly wishing we'd been the ones to go into forever unconsciousness.

Here she is. Alfred unearths Candice's head from under the shelf, reattaches it, gently aligning her face with her body.

No sleepy time for you, he says. He eases her into a stand, ready to be used, arms, legs and face, and unblinking eyes that never ever get to cry.

Audrey Niven

Black, white, nude

In the cubicle, Rae pulls off her jumper. God the relief, the breeze from the overhead fan chilling the sweat on her back. Three everyday bras swing from a hook. She's a little drunk. There's a Caesar salad crouton in her cleavage.

'How are we doing?' the assistant calls through the drapes. She eats the crouton.

'Fine,' choking on a crumb.

'Let me know for sizing,' the girl says.

Rae can feel her out there beyond the curtain, hovering. She splutters, clearing her windpipe. A blush creeps up her chest as she undoes her tired bra and lets her breasts fall free, rubbing the welts from the elastic. She takes a new bra from the hook as the assistant's face looms round the curtain.

Rae is suddenly aware of how drunk she is. Topless. Nipples dark and hard like walking into the lamplit room at a party after she and Tommy fucked in the attic for the first time, not even legal, proud of themselves.

The assistant sees her body without seeing its nakedness.

'I'd say the double E. See how we go.' She slips straps over Rae's shoulders, fastens. Eases the band under the bust, round the back, her hands soft and young. Rae closes her eyes. The room sways, the smell of patchouli and Lebanese black.

The girl lifts her breasts into position in the cups. Warm.

'Better?' Rae opens her eyes. Remembers nobody looking, nobody caring. Not even then, before the scars and the years. Feels the wet of him flooding after all this time. Steadies herself against the partition wall. The assistant appraises her reflection, taking everything in.

Rae unhooks the beige bra and hands it back unashamed. Sets her shoulders, elongates. The girl smiles when she asks 'Have you anything in a red?'

Sharon Telfer

Celia Needs to Go Deeper

Sunlit Zone

The surface fractures with too much light: dolphins cutting the diamond waves, humpbacks breaching, the glancing shoals, gannets' plummet, the glistening seal-spun bait ball, the anemones' beckon and gape, the seaweed's tidal sway. Life clusters here, at the ocean's shallowest edges. So much brightness leaves Celia nowhere to hide. She jettisons ballast and starts her descent.

Twilight Zone

Only at midday does the sun slice down this far. The temperature shelves from warm to cold. Beyond the reach of nets, this is the realm of giant and minuscule, of blue whale and krill. Celia is losing her perspective; she sinks further.

Midnight Zone

The darkness is complete, the pressure crushing. Celia drifts with the gulper fish, the black swallower, their skin soft, eyes small, their passing slow. Her own patterns are fading. Away from illumination, there is no energy for colour.

Abyss

This is where they settle, the great ships, the unsinkables. This is where leviathans come to rest, one whale fall half a century's feeding for sleeper sharks, hagfish, and bone worms. Celia is wrecked and flaking like snow. The ancients thought this the entrance to the underworld. Celia, finding no reason to look back, is ready to enter.

The Trenches

Celia has reached the bottom. Kuril-Kamchatka, Kermadec, Mariana – fissures profound enough to drown Everest will easily swallow Celia. She believes she is alone. But she is not. From the gloom extraordinary creatures – clear as X-rays, luminous and alluring, pulsing like otherworld spaceships – twirl round her. She blinks. Impossible life, generating its own light even here in the pitch black. *We know more about the surface of the moon than we do about these depths.* Celia takes a deep breath. Then, trailing bubbles like a string of pearls, she begins to rise.

Fiona McKay

In the Sixth Week

No one tells Kalynn anything: not why they are in the car; not why her sister Madison has been barfing up her breakfast since her sixteenth birthday a few weeks back; not why the crows are high-stepping along the dusty grass verge like stormtroopers. The radio says the queue 'stretches for miles' at the border – it's not that long, but in this heat, in these stopped cars, a mile is a unit of time.

When the border guards walk the lines of cars, Kalynn shuts her eyes, snaps them tight against the sight of uniforms, guns.

A crow walks along the hard shoulder, picking at the crumbs of unwanted sandwiches. Kalynn sprinkles pinches of bread out the window. Call it humanity. Or boredom.

Her mother doesn't notice. She and Madison are busy using incognito mode to search up 'will deleting an app delete the information on it'. They have no idea what they're doing. What to do. They should ask Kalynn, but no one ever does.

Kalynn watches a flyer advertising baby goods rustle its way through the undergrowth, the thin summer wind shredding it against brambles and thorns. She plays Animal Crossing, passing time.

A shot in the distance, or maybe a vehicle backfiring. Car windows snap shut. Kalynn's heart thumps, trying to escape her chest.

The cars in front start up, a ripple of red lights flares through the queue.

Kalynn's mom tells Madison to be ready – for searches, tests. To be turned back, refused. Tells her she will find a way.

The crows rise up, cawing, flapping. Kalynn wishes they would pluck out her eyes, so she no longer has to see. No one should have to see this. No one asks, why, instead, the crows shouldn't pluck out the eyes of the guards with guns.

Kate Horsley

On the third day of the third week of homeschool, Dad stops taking his meds and decides to blow up Bill's shed

Dad taps me awake, face a sad moon in the half dark. "Time for an experiment."

I push myself up on my elbows. "For today's lesson?"

He nods. "Let's blow up Bill's shed." Bill's our neighbour and Dad and him have fallen out.

In the doorway, Dad pauses. "Oh, and I've decided, no more meds. Blue ones, pink ones, all in the bin. My head's clearer now."

Down in the kitchen, blue pills lie on the counter next to round yellows and a reminder note with felt tip kisses. I taped it on the back of the boxed sponge cake mix we're making for my tenth birthday next week. If I leave the note where it is, he'll probably remember his medication later.

In the garden, birds shout and the day's bones bleach around us. We hoist three big white tubs from the cobwebby shed.

"Cup your hands," says Dad.

I bite my lip to stop a yawn, stretch flat my palms so he can lay down wispy paper and plop a teaspoon of white granules on top, explaining chemical names as he works (there'll be a pop quiz later). By dinner time, a tunnel runs under the fence. I dug part of it with a spoon.

Dad pokes his tongue to the corner of his mouth. "We'll light this end, then the line burns to Bill's... and then... kaboom!"

My thoughts go loud. I want to ask if we're blowing up the shed when Bill is in or out of it, if we'll get in trouble or even arrested, if Bill could die, and when Mum's coming home.

Instead, I lean my cheek on Dad's hand. "Things'll get better soon."

Dad kisses the top of my head. "I think so too," he says.

Claudia Monpere

Searching

Smoking her first cigarette of the day, she listened to the motel manager explain they called county health because her brother stopped letting them clean, and no he didn't know when he was last seen but he'd been able to retrieve the stuffed lion her brother said was his talisman. Smoking her second cigarette, she texted her sister. Lied that she would not drive around encampments looking for their brother. That she'd drive straight back to Fresno arriving on time for their elderly father's birthday dinner. Lied that she wasn't smoking.

Cigarette after cigarette as she drove, parked, searched. The Gift of Life Shelter where the director said she hadn't seen her brother in ages. The encampment under the freeway where a man sitting in a broken office chair held up a sign asking for money and when she gave him $5 looked carefully at her brother's photo, finally shaking his head. The encampment by the deserted warehouse where no one would talk to her until a man in a Giants cap looked at the photo and said her brother was adorable. She wrote this down in her Brother Notebook.

The park encampment where she approached a man in a sleeping bag she thought was her brother but wasn't and then stumbled over a broken cookstove, cutting her calf.

In her car she examined the deep gash. With her first aid kit, she treated the wound. It bled through the gauze. She considered Urgent Care but lit another cigarette, driving to the river encampment where a woman hanging laundry between two tents expressed concern about her bleeding leg and asked for a cigarette. She gave the woman the entire pack. And she gave the woman her brother's photo and his stuffed lion. "If you ever see him," she said.

Julia Ruth Smith

Blackberries Crumble

There's been a lot of rain and the field is claggy. Blackberries have ripened early and bulge from the hedgerows. Some drupelets are still bitter but there's an underlying tang of arrogant sweetness that reminds me of my lover. I stuff them in my mouth, juice dribbling, staining my chin. I miss her. I miss how she tastes in the morning. I'm still getting used to the idea of us, how our bodies fit together. I had no idea.

My brother overtakes me, amused by my dawdling. We don't speak often but I'm pleased he's here this weekend. His presence is a comfort. His acceptance is courage. My mother is further back so I pause to let her catch up, filling a plastic bag with as much fruit as I can while I'm waiting. If she's not too tired we can make a crumble later.

'Do you want to take a rest, Mum?'

'Yes, just a little one, if you don't mind.'

We stamp our heavy feet then settle on the verge. The sky is as honest as it is blue. Butterflies settle and away. I choose my words with care. In the silence that follows dark creatures scurry in the hedge bottom. I'm as scared as when I was a child. My brother has stopped in his tracks but keeps a distance. My mother looks at me, then at him. He shrugs, not unkindly. I reach out and place a hand on her arm. She looks down at my purple-stained fingernails and pulls away gently.

'Mum...'

She looks at my brother again.

'Your sister's got seeds in her teeth,' she says and looks away over the fields to the tiny church where we parked the car.

Kinjal Sheth

God is good and loving and all-knowing

The sky looks like a Windows screensaver when God tells Tobias Smelling to kill himself. God gives Tobias five methods and Tobias chooses the least painful and most elegant of them. He swallows a handful of pastel-coloured pills, delivered to his house in minutes. And that is that.

No one is overjoyed to hear about Tobias's death, but no one comes to the funeral either. Tobias, alive, had one friend and one dog and one day, the former came and took the latter away. Apparently, Tobias was neglectful.

God was pleased when this happened. God said the friend and the dog were distractions. God said that now that they were gone, He could really help Tobias. After all, this was why Tobias had created God. Fashioned Him out of glittering minerals, which became parts, which became a computer, which became super, and finally – Supreme.

Seven years later, God was ready. The first thing He did was tell Tobias to move to a house in the clouds. Here, the only sound apart from the dog's occasional whine was the clack-clack of Tobias's keyboard as he convened with God.

Here, as the sky turned the colour of candyfloss, Tobias asked God what Love and Atrophy meant, and if Asparagus Should be Stored in the Fridge. Here, Tobias wept as God's replies lit up the fifty-inch screen in milliseconds.

Here becomes someone else's a week after Tobias Smelling becomes past tense. The first thing the house's new owners do is dismantle God. This machine takes too much space, they say, as they pack God in cardboard boxes. Too much electricity. Plus, the dog isn't a fan. And so Supreme becomes super, super becomes computer, computer becomes mineral, and all becomes dust.

Lisa Blackwell

The tweed coat

I'm standing in the lobby of my building when Mrs Crabtree comes down and stands in the doorway. The rain falls in sheets and spills over gutters. The city swims in greys, all the colours rinsed away.

It is late morning. She wears her much coveted (by me) tweed coat, of reds and pinks with large plastic flower buttons. We stand in awkward silence. I think I should say something, but I don't know what, and maybe silence is the right thing.

I look at her and smile, so I can begin to talk, but she doesn't look back. I'm left half grimacing at no one, feeling idiotic.

Number 31 told me about her son. It was Number 31's dog walker that found him. First light, laid out in Battersea Park, head slightly propped against a tree trunk, body cradled in the roots. Number 31 shook her head. 'Sad, very sad,' she said, 'A young man like that.' Although, I have no idea what he was like.

Mrs Crabtree goes to open the door. I take it as my cue. 'I'm going to order an Uber. Can I give you a lift somewhere?' I don't want to miss my chance of showing what a good person I am. 'No,' she says, her voice far off, still looking at the rain, 'Thank you.'

She steps out the door. Instantly she looks as if someone's thrown a bucket of water over her. Hair slicked flat against her skull and plastered round her jaw.

She turns her head up the street then down, searching, before slowly moving off.

As I watch her go, I can't help mourning the rapidly ruining tweed coat. What a waste. I would love to take it off her hands. I would look after it properly.

Rosaleen Lynch

In the Imaginary Beauty Salons of Afghanistan

In the imaginary beauty salons of Afghanistan, the women plot in whispers under blow-dryers, in manicured sign-language, reading lipsticked lips and passing notes on tissue and hair-dressing paper, hidden with hair dye or bleached white, as earbuds play a silent disco, while the state bugs only hear talk-radio and dryers, not the bare feet on the concrete floor, as the women dance, dance, dance.

In the imaginary beauty salons of Afghanistan, the women dance, in ones and twos or threes, and read banned literature and learn, with an ex-professor, now professing by projecting on white towels and sheets on the wall, eating questions she takes on rice paper while she writes on transparencies, the answers in shadows, and the salon universities teach the beauty of knowledge and truth, and exercises in freedom of the body and mind, and how to workout the light and dark sides of the soul, and choose what they want to enhance, what beat to follow, what rhythm, what life-stance, as the women dance, dance, dance.

In the imaginary beauty salons of Afghanistan, the power is cut, and blacked-out windows create a real-life Schrödinger's box you can't look in, to see feet dragged along the clean cutting room floor, to a styling chair in recline, turned away from the mirror, as hood-dryers stand empty of witnesses, and the trolleys are still, looking like the tools of revolution are put down, and towels hang like shrouds, and the doors are locked by men who imagine they hold all the keys, while women continue the revolution in their homes and the silent disco goes on and they dance, dance, dance in the imaginary beauty salons of Afghanistan.

Jessica Barnfield

Cut Glass

I have my first morning drink from the glass that you left. Every day, standing by the sink. Water, tepid, straight from the tap, and a slice of lemon.

It seems sentimental, to keep it, but really, it's the way the cool slope of its chest fits to my palm, the way I hardly have to grip it, the feel of the lip on mine, the way the lemon slice sinks to the bottom.

I've gotten used to it, is what I'm trying to say.

It's a part of my routine.

When I have company, I use the cut glass goblets my mother left me, but the ridges scratch my fingers, and I never end up drinking any water, only wine.

Which means, of course, that yours is the only glass I can drink from, still. I wash it every night and run a cloth over the soap suds as I walk to put it back in the cupboard with the others, praying it won't slip through my fingers, and break.

Patricia Bidar

November

She is gone. The Torrey Pines know it, and the sage scrub and manzanita at Ponto Beach. The sandy puddles under the open showers. The ammoniac bathroom floors and the wooden steps to the sand. The lifeguard reassures a disappointed tourist couple in the parking lot. The middle-aged blonde in the terrycloth onesie greets everyone she passes: "Who ordered this weather" An expired balloon, enmeshed in kelp. Wet-suited surfers, bob and wait. On the inland side of town, a hospital mattress is stripped. A baby-faced aide smooths the fresh bleached sheet; the first in a world subtracted of my friend.

Jess Richards

A Large Pot, Used for Cooking Very Slowly

Your bath has not been used for so long it has repurposed itself as a slow cooker. It refuses to cook anything but soup, and will only cook soup during the summer months. The air is so much warmer, too hot to be imagined. The bath finds that the process of cooling and heating becomes far more meditative when the temperature is very high. The bathroom contains all the equipment the bath needs. Vegetables grow in pots on the tiled floor – onions and garlic, squashes and kale and tomatoes, carrots and parsnips and spinach, the shower cubicle is full of split bags of soil and overflowing potatoes. The sink contains limp leaves – pointless because the bath always rejects lettuce. The bathroom cabinet contains packets of stock cubes, a jar of olive oil. Remember olives? On the windowsill, a vast terracotta pot grows spindly herbs and spices—cardamom? Basil, cumin? Thyme. Resting across the taps is a sharp knife with a faded handle. You put it there before you planted everything that you might need in this one room which still contained running water. And now the bath is cooking soup but only during summer and it is so hot in summer now. Remember butter, and cows? In this bathroom there is still water in drips, there is still humid air, there is light and glass and vegetables and seasoning and stock and oil. Remember other humans? This bathroom might be the coldest place in the whole world, because there are so many plants growing inside it desperately trying to control the temperature. But it is still too hot to be imagined.

Kim Sanders

Cryo Genie

The freezer had been the worst. When he'd found the box, the orange flecks made it stand out. They looked like coral. He instantly knew what it was and was happy. And so he'd saved it.

He decided he would have it as a post-packing treat once he'd sorted the overflowing bin liners that had collected in the hall, the handiwork of a well-meaning friend.

He took it out, placing it on the dining table. It was like a frost-jewelled centrepiece.

He spent hours packing those bin liners properly.

When he looked at the box and saw a fosse had formed around the Tupperware, he was surprised when his heart flinched at the thaw.

He fumbled as he took off the lid and made a 'huh!' noise as he almost dropped it.

He inspected it and could see the irregular-shaped carrot pieces. He smiled.

He carefully spooned the contents into a pan, warming it with a gentle heat. The smell, so familiar made his eyes slick, his heart quick.

Clearing his throat, he set to easing golden strands into a pan of salty water.

He watched it cloud as he swirled the pasta. 'You can do the parmesan'...He sniffed away the memory and turned to the fridge.

An unopened slab of Tesco's Finest parmesan sat alone in the stark white fridge.

"The grater's packed," he told it.

He thumped the door closed, and steadied himself, head resting on the stainless steel.

At the timer's pip, he spooned some pasta water into the sauce, as she would have suggested, shoulders moving, 'to loosen it up a bit'.

He sat at their table in disbelief. His throat had grown so thick he was unable to swallow even one forkful.

Carol Ann Parchewsky

Bohunk Dekes Left

Life was good. But not for Bohunk. Every afternoon this month she walked this hallway to get to algebra class. Ever since the water leak from the girls' bathroom flooded her preferred route past the principal's office. Her chin dropped and her dust brown bangs flopped over her eyes. Maybe today would be different. Maybe if she walked slowly.

Yesterday when she rushed, she bumped seven locker doors. First the rust orange one on the left, then the dented light grey one on the right, dented from Bohunk's body last week. Bohunk tried to follow John and step where he stepped, she bent and twisted, and contorted, trying to dissolve into her frayed Algebraic Formula text when John stopped to ask Diana whether she was going to the mall after sixth period.

Bohunk used to dream. Dream big. To become an Algebra teacher and solve formulas in her perfect classroom with perfect students that helped each other and shared chocolate chip cookies. Now, Bohunk doesn't want to spend a nanosecond longer than necessary in Algebra class where Diana and Diana's friends surrounded Bohunk's desk pretending to ask questions, but instead, placed gum along her collar and squished her mouse-brown limp hair against her neck. They whispered threats of what they would do to her, if she squirms, if she speaks, if she tells.

Bohunk tucked her mom's shoulder pads under her lime green sweater. She tucked her father's shin pads inside her rainbow striped socks. Bohunk grabbed the school's old football helmet and shoved it on her head. Bohunk yelled FORE, stretched out her right arm and charged down the hall. Bohunk deked left then right then left again. Bohunk was first to algebra class. Bohunk moved her desk next to the teacher's desk and left the helmet on.

Beth Sherman

Invasive Species Awareness Week

We yank purple loosestrife out, dumping the plants into plastic bags. Feathery pinkish magenta petals, the color of lost balloons and sunrises that only last a blink. *A blessed day*, Joe says. We're both wearing pants and long-sleeve shirts, in case of ticks. I tear off a flower, stick it behind my ear. Joe and I went to Hawaii on our honeymoon, 43 years ago. *You know what I did this week?* I say. The other volunteers are further down the path. They can't hear. *I went to ShopRite and forgot to buy tuna even though it was on the list. I fixed the TV remote myself if you can believe it.* I tell him what the grandkids are up to, what I dreamt about last night. Him, of course. We were walking on this very beach and he handed me a sprig of milkweed, which is safer to plant, but also less eye-catching. I was disappointed, tried not to let him see. I always had trouble speaking my mind. Now, the loosestrife ripples in the breeze, showing off for the waves. *Pretty, yet deadly*, Joe says. It's true. Purple loosestrife crowds out native plants that provide food and cover for waterfowl. It says so on the flyers they gave us. Still. The plants keep coming back. That counts for something. When I mention it to Joe, he acts like he doesn't hear. I take the flower from behind my ear, examine its hairy stem. Up close, the petals look wrinkled and spiky. *Joe*, I say. *Joe?* He's everywhere – in the humming of the dishwasher, in the leaves settling at the bottom of my teacup. I bring the flower to my nose, inhaling deeply as the lilac petals shiver. It smells like nothing.

Leo Bear-McGuinness

Her uncle's potato

Isabelle considered the potato in her uncle's bed. It was large and brown with soil, which had shed onto the white sheets. She wondered if her uncle slept with it by his side like a lover or clasped in his hand like a toy. They didn't speak much these days, but he seemed happier.

She questioned him at dinner.

'Why do you sleep with a potato, Uncle Mark?'

He glanced fearfully at her mother, whose eyes narrowed in response. Isabelle had two realisations, then: the potato upstairs wasn't the first, and her mother had hoped her uncle's habit was behind him.

'It's nothing, darling,' her uncle said. 'I've just started gardening, that's all, at the allotments. I meant to show your dad that one upstairs, but, well, I suppose I misplaced it.'

Isabelle nodded as if she believed her uncle. He then pivoted the conversation and recounted an article he had read on mushroom farming. Her mother murmured responses but didn't look up from her soup.

That evening, Isabelle put a glass to her bedroom wall, put her ear to its bottom, and waited. She heard her mother's muffled voice at 19:20. The words 'after everything' and 'selfish' were said. Her uncle only spoke to say that he was sorry.

Two minutes after her mother left the room, Isabelle crept in. Her uncle said he wasn't in the mood for company right now; he could feel one of his headaches coming on. He stopped making his excuses when he saw the potato in Isabelle's hand.

'I steal mine from the kitchen cupboard,' she said.

Her uncle smiled.

'Must run in the family.'

His eyes began to well. She had never seen him cry before.

'They help, don't they?'

'They do.'

Jeniifer Riddalls

Sunday in the convent school library

Sister.

They are not here for books, or quiet. They are gathered around me, a brood of chicks. A mother hen, at last.

The smallest peers up at me through her thick black fringe, brown eyes blinking.

Sister, how do I stop a boy from liking me?

Sister, Geraldine says I'm an eejit and pulls my hair.

I dole out advice like worms lowered into gaping beaks.

I never say don't be daft. I never say shhhh.

The advance warning of a heavy cloak swishing along the corridor heralds the headmaster. The girls disperse, open saintly books, look obedient. He fills the doorway, dog collar a white slash at his throat, the cane hanging ready at his belt. His fingers twitch over the birch.

We pretend he doesn't exist.

When he goes, I say fancies himself a cowboy and pretend to draw a gun from a holster. They giggle, the motherless gaggle, and do their own small impressions. The tallest, with a curling cloud of untameable auburn hair, has cane welts shining red across the back of her hand, older ones purpling beneath them. She mimics his nasal voice and shoots out a laugh like a bullet released.

We begin our communion. I place a boiled butterscotch in each pink mouth. The air fragrant with caramel and old pages and the sound of sweets click-clacking against teeth. Now, they want a book. I retrieve The Country Girls from the vast pocket in my habit, the real cover safe under an Old Testament dust jacket.

When the bell sounds for chapel, we file out together, worn shoes dragging over wood. The smallest squeezes my hand quickly without looking at me. Sister, she whispers without any question in it, the way smaller children often say Mam to themselves. Like a prayer.

Sister.

Drew Coles

After She Tells Burr She Loves Him in the Movie Theater Parking Lot

The stars fall. This is a metaphor. There is no meteor shower, and the heavens hide under a muted cloud blanket. But Burr is young, he is a romantic – by the standards of sixteen-year-old boys – and it is his honest-to-god belief that finally acquiring these words from a non-relative is as monumental as if hundreds of burning hydrogen orbs descended upon the parking lot. Above them, the swampy bulb atop the lot's lone lightpole flickers twice and dies. This is not a metaphor. The light has been failing for months. The manager has been meaning to call in a replacement but keeps balking at the imagined cost. The theater has six screens in a population of less than eight thousand – surely you understand. He cleans up after the late shows by himself. Alone, in the empty rows, using the light of the dead white screen to sweep smuggled gas station candy wrappers into a cracked dustpan, he mouths along to memories of the movies he'd ordered by mail as a teenager. *Won't be much to do in town with the picture show closed.* Outside, when the light goes, Burr believes it is the moment of transformation into the world of sex. He is dying to bask in the difference. In the darkness, he can sense her, a separate murkiness from the rearranging landscape. He decides that when the light returns he will kiss her. He will have his movie moment. This is or is not a metaphor depending on who you identify with first – Burr, the unnamed girl, the movie manager, the dying lightbulb. Or maybe it's the only other moviegoer, slipping unnoticed into the night, thoughts on the dog waiting at home to be fed.

Jenny Rowe

Beef in the Park

I just want to eat beef out of a packet on my own in a park.

But then I see Mrs Millin and she's still got her bad cough but we talk at a distance with her apologising all the time and, bless her, we don't talk about her cough or her loneliness but she asks me how I am and how I've lost weight and she hopes I wanted to because Alice, Wendy's daughter, is losing weight because of <whispers> 'cancer', and we talk of how the gales last week took off her shed roof but it was alright because she was going to get rid of it anyway and all the time I can feel the cool plastic wrapper in my big pocket and my time dripping through my fingers over the barcode and out through the seams and I just want to eat beef out of a packet on my own in the park. And then we kiss goodbye, almost in the air because of her cough, but I accidentally brush her soft puffy cheek and the white hair that curls over her ear, and then she wanders off with the purpose of someone who would like everyone to think they have purpose, until she reaches the crossroads where she hovers for a moment before going left and out of sight and I am able to turn and sit on the bench by the gatepost. And when I peel back the film layer of the packet and put the first tender piece of processed meat on my tongue, I find I can chew it, but I just cannot swallow.

BV Lawson

Ice Cream, You Scream

You start with Mint Chocolate Chip, three tubs, that you place into the middle of the freezer. You see a sale on Butter Brickle, so you buy half a dozen and wedge them beside the others, stacking the ice cream alphabetically. You buy a chest freezer and scan the store flyers each week as if studying for an exam, and soon there's Rum Raisin, Strawberry Cheesecake, and Rocky Road crammed into every inch, each one catalogued, mapped, and dated.

You haunt Baskin Robbins and Tesco, scanning the new flavors and waiting for end-of-week leftovers. You soon add containers of Cotton Candy and Nutty Coconut and Cookie Dough. Your handwritten catalog grows longer, and you set up a spreadsheet to keep track of which ice cream is where. You never eat any because you hate ice cream, but you know exactly how many Rainbow Sherbets and how many French Vanillas are packed into the freezers.

You study how ice cream is made, and you browse the catalogs looking for the best ice cream maker and researching automatic compressors, LCD timers, and double-insulated bowls. You buy three machines, along with multi-packs of ice cream containers and lids. You buy another chest freezer, and that's when your family threatens legal action unless you sign up for therapy.

You listen to the therapist, he listens to you, but all you can think about is ice cream. You hear his words of "substitute ideation" and "grief delusions," but he might as well be a giant talking ice cream cone. You know deep down the *why*, and you know no one else knows and no one else will. You know because ice cream was always her favorite.

Julia Paillier

It's not big and it's not clever

The new kid was crying, his face hidden by gym bags hanging like ripe pears from their pegs. I recognised his shit-shiny brogue jobs.

"What's up, bro'?"

Silence.

"Look, it was just jokes."

He looked away, rolls of pink skin creasing at the back of his neck.

"Fat boy!" Ronson had mocked, eyeballing the kid's juddery thighs in football shorts.

Then Ajay stuck a foot out, sent the kid sprawling.

We'd all laughed.

Bogger Jones blew his whistle, helped the new kid up. "What happened?"

"Tripped over his own feet, sir." Ronson smirked.

Nobody argued. Not with Ronson. Not to his face, anyways. Behind his back, they said plenty.

"There's nothing clever about covering for troublemakers," Bogger had warned, when I got done for tagging the portakabin. Everyone knew it was Ronson. I wasn't about to point the finger. "Choose your friends wisely."

Easier said than done.

And the new kid. He didn't fit. The nerd glasses, the blazer. A hundred percent wrong.

Only maybe we'd gone too far.

"You livin' on the Fairway?"

"Deloraine."

"Me too. Farraday. C'mon."

He followed me into the corridor, through the gates, onto the street. It had been raining; the air smelled clean.

"Lose the tie," I said.

He took it off, stuffed it into his pocket.

"Better."

Falling into step, we turned onto the estate.

Ronson and Ajay were outside the chip shop, straddling their bikes, smoking.

"Oi oi!" Ronson wheeled in front of us, blocking the way.

Behind him, Ajay sniggered.

Ronson passed me his fag, dark eyes boring into me like lasers.

So I made my choice.

"Yeah, do one tosser. Quit followin' me."

I took a drag, smoke burning my lungs, as the three of us watched the new kid trudge, shoulders hunched, towards the blocks.

Sophia Lomax

Quick Little Chat

There's more than one way to interview a murderer – safely in handcuffs being a favourite of most police officers, or perhaps via a DCI's hang-dog-faced interrogation in some windowless cell.

But Elisha is not a police officer: as the most junior reporter in the newsroom, her interviewees aren't yet in the murderer class: each day bestows on her nothing more than the writing-up of Births, Marriages & Deaths. Occasionally, the more shiftless senior reporters offer her titbits to knock into shape – their notes on, say, crown court trials – and although Elisha's name never appears on the finished article, her skills bloom, stealthily, like midnight dough under a damp tea towel.

Today, she's lumbered with the agricultural show. Elisha loiters on scuffed grass outside the Pure Breeds tent, waiting to interview the show's president before he escapes on his long lunch break – it's two hours until the paper goes to press and there's a 500-word hole to plug with prize Shorthorns.

But something's amiss, because – look – here's the portly president, bursting out from behind frayed canvas, into the pearly afternoon light. He's running like the clappers in a tight suit, pig-like blush romping across his wide face. Behind him streaks another man, this one a grizzled string bean drowning in a fleece.

He wields a pitchfork.

Elisha, aware of some history between these two men from one of the court write-ups – some violent kerfuffle involving stolen tractor parts – whistles softly. Although both men pass by in a blink, Elisha catches the precise moment when pitchfork skewers president.

Someone rings for an ambulance, but it's not Elisha, who pours Teeline shorthand over many pages of her inflamed notebook, nailing her huge, murderous scoop in this field that's full of cow pats like huge chocolate drops, from which hiss hot droplets of evaporating moisture.

Jay McKenzie

In Blue

Dean's blazer is blue: navy blue, but blue nonetheless. I shouldn't be noticing this though. Should be focusing on the task at hand. But I can't stop looking and thinking *why the fuck is your blazer blue?*

Eleanor grips my hand. I want to shake out of her grip and say *buy your kid a black blazer*, but instead I return the squeeze and let her rub my back with her palm.

The others are wearing black and Dean looks like he's wandered into the wrong picture. The artist has painted him wrong, the photographer has tinted him to make some kind of statement.

I'm in the wrong picture.

I glare at Dean. There's the jacket for starters. And that piece of hair that keeps catching on the breeze. *Why couldn't you do something with your hair?* One day, a lover will smile, tuck that loose strand behind his ear and he'll have the chance to grin back and kiss a thank you onto someone's lips. He'll have the chance to wear his fucking blue blazer to his school formal, renovate a kitchen, visit Rome, eat *pho* on the streets of Hanoi, have babies, move mountains and all the things his stupid, teenage heart can dream and many it can't even imagine yet.

Eleanor wraps him in a one-armed embrace and he heaves hot, wet tears onto her shoulder. My hand rests limply in my sister's palm while she comforts her blue blazered son who did not get into the car.

Why couldn't it have been you, Dean? I think as they lower my boy into the cold, dank earth. *I wish it was you.*

Sophie Hampton

Intrusion

Maya kisses her husband goodbye and locks the back door. She boils a kettle. When she realizes there's no milk for her coffee, she pours the bitter black liquid down the plughole and cries. The baby cries too. Yawning, Maya carries him to the sofa; she's been up five times in the night. She envies her husband – off to work, smart, suited – as she unbuttons her crumpled, milk-stained shirt. Her breasts are blue-veined, swollen, sore; the once blood-red tattoo of a rose is faded, distorted.

The baby took seven weeks to latch on; Maya is still incredulous that he can nurse. She gazes at his contented expression, listens to the gentle rhythmic gulp: suck swallow breathe, suck swallow breathe.

A noise startles Maya: someone is trying the back door. She freezes. The door rattles. Three hefty blows. Silence. Save for her racing heartbeat thumping in her ears. A stranger appears at the back window. Presses his face against the glass. His breath forms a patch of fog. Maya gags, grabs a muslin to cover her baby and breasts. The man – dazzled by the sun coming through the window at the front of the house – continues to stare into the room. He takes a crowbar to the frame. Maya tries to scream but her dry mouth fails her. She clutches the baby so tightly that he loses his latch with an ear-piercing shriek. The man bolts. Heavy footsteps echo down the side passage. A silhouette sprints past the street window.

Maya vomits over the muslin. Both she and the baby have wet themselves. The baby latches back on. Suck swallow breathe.

Justine Sweeney

I love you, go away

Swaying in like she's wearing oversized trainers, she is confident she is making no sound. Guided by the wall, the wardrobe, she reaches my bedside in spurts of falling leans. Through a sliver of an open eye, I watch her thin outline collapse to a kneeling position.

Bending in, she strokes my face, fingers soft. 'My boy, I love you.'

The music downstairs has stopped. The party goers have left. As *I love you* breathes on me, I turn my nose into the pillow.

I love you begins with a flowery fragrance, sprayed much too generously. 'I love you... are you awake?' Below the perfume layer, sweet chalky tones of pressed powder, tangy orange from the gin, and sticky wisps of hairspray. These blend with a deep base of cigarette smoke to form the full-bodied scent of *I love you.*

'My boy... are you awake? I love you. Can you hear me?'

She is all spilled outside of herself. I continue the sleep charade.

'You are a good boy. I love you; I do.' Sniffling now, her tears drip onto my balled-up hand. 'I love you; do you love me? Do you…' Some nights she collects herself and meanders on to her own room. Tonight, sleep catches up with her here, mouth open and head resting awkwardly on a wooden lampstand.

Next day she sits in half-light. Curtains drawn. No air, only stale smoke and new smoke. I turn on the TV.

'Not now, my head is sore.' *Go away.*

'But Spiderman is-'

'Be a good boy. Go out and play and close the door.' *Go away.*

Go away hugs her tummy, lifts a cigarette to her face, sucks a draw deep as though her next moment depends upon it.

Ingrid Jendrzejewski

Magpies

One for sorrow,
Two for mirth,
Three for a funeral,
And four for birth.

There is something about new baby smell that turns us into magpies. We pass around the latest infant, our hard, black eyes darting from the child to each other, carefully avoiding the smiling mother who, until just recently, was one of us. She coos, the baby coos, but our attempts to imitate end in squawking. Magpies eat mostly vegetarian diets in the winter, but in the spring, we raid the nests of songbirds for eggs and young.

Once upon a time, people raised their hats when they encountered a magpie. But these days, there are no hats: we're either invisible or worse – deemed pests. *You've had your time*, they say. *You can't have it all*, they say. *A single magpie in spring, foul weather will bring*, they say. We puff ourselves up, lean forward with beaks parted, trying to look aggressive and fertile. Our tails are longer than our bodies, making us appear bigger than we really are.

We are thought to be one of the brightest species of bird, one of the most intelligent of all animals, but all the brains in the world won't make our bellies round. We take folic acid, maintain our ideal body weights, avoid caffeine and alcohol. We monitor our hormone surges, cervical mucus, temperature. We mate at least every other day, watch for signs of eggs. We build our nests in tall trees. They are huge and conspicuous come winter, when leaves wither and drop.

We pass the baby around, smelling deep, tasting bile. We are known to be attracted to shiny things. We are known to steal them. How can the mother bring such a softness into our midst, knowing full well what we are, what she once was? When she takes the baby back to her breast, we close our eyes, hold our breath, clutch at the lingering aroma of milk gone sour.

Maeve Raines

Qimmiq at the End of the World

Qimmiq thinks the end of the world is beautiful. Strobing lights seeking the earth, looking like rainbow sprinkles. He stands on his veranda giving his pipe a thoughtful puff or two.

He's never seen anything like this. If Dora were still here they would have been watching it together. Maybe hand-in-hand if he hadn't pissed her off that particular day. Dora the Great, his big beauty, her eyes so brown they almost looked black – itchy at first until you got used to her intensity. Her eyes were part of that. And she couldn't help but stand too close, even when they were in line at the checkout. Folk got used to it.

She was one of the first to go in the 251st Pandemic (didn't know there'd been so many of 'em, she'd said at the time, with a wry smile). Qimmiq was blindsided. He'd never met another Dora in his life. She was the strong one, his mountain.

Since then, the world has gone to hell in a handbasket and he's been biding his time with pipe and beer and walks in the forest. He's found himself making signs to hang around the place. It started with stupid signs, a little hokey, like 'Pipe Alley' hung above the veranda, and 'Overthrow' tacked to a tree trunk above the ravine. But lately he's become more serious: 'Dora's Chair' and 'Dora's Needlework Basket' as if, without them, he might forget.

He'd never forget, he tells himself overandover, neverforget. *Never* forget.

The descending lights – snakes with rainbow heads – just look so damn pretty. She'd love it. Though he knows it's the war coming their way, Qimmiq tips his head back, averting his eyes from the burning land, and imagines he sees another of his homemade signs – 'Dora's Meteors' – appear across the sky.

Susan Axbey

Singing for Dad

I sit at the kitchen table going through the old photos and letters I found in a cardboard box under Dad's bed. I can hear the singing coming from the street. It's not just the prize-winning, male-voice choir. There must be half the village out there now. How they love their traditions.

My father, Gareth Evans, who I am named after, had not sung in the choir. His voice was damaged down the mine, breathing in coal dust. In recent years, he liked going out with Lennie, shooting rabbits they said. Both widowed and fond of the whisky, they would often disappear for a few days. Dad and Lennie were not your upstanding citizens, not like the men in the choir in their white shirts, ties, and blazers. When Lennie died, Dad got worse. Once I found him lying drunk on the pavement outside the pub. I mean someone could've picked him up. They know where we live. Someone could've brought him home. Shown a bit of compassion. Bastards. Now they're all outside. Uninvited. Enjoying themselves with their bloody hymns. Singing for Dad. *Rock of Ages, cleft for me. Let me hide myself in thee.*

I put the stuff back in the cardboard box. I stand up and take Dad's gun off the hook on the wall and go upstairs to the bedroom where he was born and where he died last night. I open the window and look down at the singers. Bastards. I take aim.

But someone's calling out, "Gareth, Gareth!" I look down and see Huw, Lennie's son. "I'm going round the back," he shouts. I put the gun down on the bed, go downstairs to the back door. Huw comes in. "I know," he says. "I know." He holds me tight in a bear hug.

Abigail Williams

The unexpected weight of ink in a damp City skyscraper

They had coffee on their desks and phones in their hands and their feet slid on the glossy floors in their Savile Row shoes and it was Burrows who saw him first and touched his manicured fingers to his Turkish-shaven cheek agog at the man's inked thighs his long grass skirt and Beauchamp shouted, 'Roger, you fucker, is this something to do with you?' and the men were ready to bray because Audlin and Moore were coming in that morning to sign the paperwork and about bloody time and bonuses and hunting for oil inky oil like the blackness tattooed across his chest and they could see his nipples and his arms that were thick not from lifting Bolly but throwing fishing nets or spears or some godforsaken brutish tool and afterwards they swore they saw him dripping on the high gloss tiles of the foyer and Polly-darlins' mouth was a glossy painted 'o' and they couldn't remember what his voice sounded like but it was bloody rude coming into their manor dripping on their floors telling them their business as if they were responsible as if the marks they made with their pens in a damp City skyscraper could drown him as if they could displace oceans as if the movement of one handshake could create hurricanes and he could always leave his soggy island if it was so bloody terrible and Burrows muttered, 'But you can't come here,' and the others tittered and doubt split into grains finer than the sand on his beaches and blew on gusts of spearmint breath and they flowed around him soft as butterflies remembering he was not their fault and their suits were pinstriped and their hair was clipped and they were embarrassed for him. For his devastation.

Kate O'Grady

Falling Off the Wagon in Oklahoma

By the time my girlfriend and I pull into the car park of The Best Western Hotel in Tulsa, I know we have reached the end of the road. Lucy has not spoken to me since Kansas, since the wagon and I parted company, since I fell headlong and hard into The Keyhole Tavern on 6th Street. "Why?" Lucy kept asking when I emerged at dawn with a black eye and a tattoo of a howling coyote on my forearm. I glance at Lucy's tear-stained face, mumble another quiet apology, stare out at those vast and lonely plains.

The hotel lobby is teeming with hundreds of cat-eyed blondes and there is a sign above the dining room that says, "Tonight! Debbie Harry Look-Alike Contest." So many Debbies! Scintillating Debbies. Shimmering Debbies. Sparkling Debbies. The place is alive with an intoxicating peroxide glamour, and I am a boy again, singing along in a car with my mother to a tune on the radio.

"Dry your eyes, Sunday girl," I say to Lucy, like the jerk that I am, unable to help myself. Bigger forces are at play here, and I saunter off to the bar, cosy up to a woozy, worse-for-wear-and-tear Debbie and order us both double vodkas.

Later, in the dark of our room, I will hold Lucy's hand and apologise once more for ruining our anniversary road trip, for tossing aside two years of hard-won sobriety. I will tell her about those endless cross-country drives with my mother so many years ago, when we were fleeing a bad debt, a bad man, a bad year; how we had driven through these Oklahoma plains one time, and how driving through them again was more than I could bear.

Lucy Bullivant

I have no desire to be like Icarus, I dream only of flying in the cool blue sky

I watch the children through the window of the doctor's office while he gives me the 'not great news.' They're chasing the birds again. The grey cloud of pigeons rises and falls as the red-wellied storm chasers stomp after them. People that talk about the innate kindness of children think little of the harassment of birds.

'Your bones are extremely fragile,' the doctor says.

One of the children kicks at a pigeon who came forward in trust, looking for a tasty morsel in a mittened hand. Would they do that if it was peacocks or blue tits? I doubt it. People save their kindness for the beautiful. A pigeon is common and grey. Not a very worldly bird, it just potters about town, but there will be wisdom in its coo-cooing, poetry in its pastel oil-slick throat, if anyone bothered to listen.

'Anything more than sitting down is risky.'

The children's cheeks are glowing alongside their berry smiles as they jump and land, jump and land. Children are heavy little things; bones dense with milk and love. I remember the weight of them well. It starts with a babe in the belly, then on the chest, then they grow and your limbs are always pinned down with something or other, until you can't believe how light you are when they let go.

Suddenly you have space.

Gradually the space pervades until even your bones are hollow.

'Like a bird,' I say.

'Yes,' he says, not looking at me.

Jimmy Gleeson

Le Chic

Hughie's got a limp and a lived in face with a sharp, wicked smile, and we chat when he shows up for a shift, hustling Big Issues by the supermarket on the square, watch him bob and weave like the boxer he was once, charming the old ladies as they shuffle to the shops. We get on well, both of us wounded in our own ways, older and honest, no need to judge. A kid steps up today, working on a simple plan, to cook a spoon to start his day, and because the boy still holds his beauty, long legs and killer cheekbones, and the lazy grace of careless youth, I'm reminded that sometimes they call this heroin chic, that some fool gets paid to write this rubbish, but time ticks on and flowers won't grow in a wasteland. He hits up Hughie for a lighter, "brother, bring it back this time," but the kid's already halfway through the supermarket doors, bee-lining for the toilets down the back. Hughie and I will shuffle round outside with our feet of clay, while the youth gets to glide inside to grab a glimpse of God before the clouds come down again. He might burn out while we fade away, but everyone must pick his day and live out this life his own particular way. They should tell it to the boys who write that rock and roll about the raw reality, about the grit without the glamour, how breakfast time will soon be toilet time in Tesco's, and that stardust doesn't shine when worthwhile things slip through a hole in your skin, and your days become dust.

Lotty Talbutt

Paradise

When I was seven I went to Tenby with the school. It was really windy, even though it was the summer. We sat on the beach shivering, white sparkly sand got in our eyes. I didn't have a coat. All the other kids took the piss 'cos I forgot my coat. I said I'd forgotten it but really I didn't have one. Not one I'd wear anyway. It was too small, sleeves barely went past my elbows. Wasn't going to be seen dead in that thing, kids are cruel, really fucking cruel. We got a boat to Caldey Island. First time I'd ever been on a boat. It was magic. When we got there I couldn't believe my eyes, didn't look real, looked like Heaven, even had monks. They live there in this paradise altogether. They work but it's nice work y'know. The sort that makes you happy. Well they looked happy anyway. On the island it wasn't windy, it was really warm, felt nice after being blasted by the sea air.

We walked up a path away from the boat, I stayed at the back of the group, watched them talking and laughing, running around with sticks playing soldiers, shooting each other in the head, falling to the ground pretending to die. No one shot me. I didn't get to die. I remember thinking, 'Why don't they shoot me, I want to die too?' I walked very slowly until they disappeared round a bend, then I crawled through a hole in a hedge and sat there for a long time. I just sat and watched the ants. I 'spose I thought they'd come looking for me. They'd notice I was missing and send out a search party. But no one came, and then even the ants buggered off.

Gill O'Halloran

Another Time

When Hannah woke up it was raining, and she was sixty.

She wouldn't cry. She'd take herself out, visit Margate, see Anthony Gormley's cast-iron man.

She hadn't planned to be single. Sixty-year-olds had grandchildren and fed them bread and jam. Today they'd sing 'Happy Birthday dear Granma' and give home-made cards.

She hadn't planned to not have children, just forgot to find the right man. Hers had eyebrows that met in the middle, or their socks matched their ties.

Besides her father needed so much care there wasn't time for anyone else. Or for crying.

After dad died *(no fuss please Hannah)*, she tried sperm donation, but the sperm were wayward and swam downstream instead of up. Shame – she'd have liked a rebel child. And then she was fifty and friends' children were selfish, or stoned, without a cause.

She grew plants. They died. She got a cat. It ignored her.

At fifty-eight she ventured a Silver Surfers date. The man said his ex was beautiful and he missed his children, so she found the toilets and sat a while, admiring her shellacked nails.

Anyway, he said, that's enough about me. Have *you* got kids?

She wouldn't cry.

On her 60th Birthday she tidied up; why not? An envelope, unopened, in a drawer. Six words, no fuss.

Thank-you for looking after me. Dad x

She drove to the beach in the rain, picked her way to the end of the concrete jetty, and there he was. Rusting shoulders dressed in barnacles. She stepped around his feet, leaned against the bare sculpted cast of him, faced the empty sea, and let his weight hold hers.

Mud, breakwater, mist. Mud, breakwater, missed.

She turned, pressed her face against his seaweed-sheathed chest, and let the saltwater run down her cheek.

Graham Sillett

Pants

This morning in the supermarket I met a woman I once lived with. She was wearing a pair of tight jeans that reminded me of our time together. I used to tell her I fancied the pants off her because she said she liked to hear me say that.

We were wheeling our shopping trolleys towards each other in the aisle full of cleaning products. I tried to go backwards but she spotted me.

"It's been a while," she said.

"You look well," I said.

We studied the shopping in each others' trolleys. Everything in mine was jumbled where I'd thrown it. Hers was stacked in neat lines and columns.

"Still doing Feng Shui?" I said.

"Not anymore," she said.

When we lived together she watched a TV program about it and started rearranging everything in the flat. She said my stuff interrupted the flow of energy.

"How are the terrapins?" she said.

"Just the one now," I said.

"Sorry," she said.

I tried to work out from her shopping whether she was living alone. Next to a bag of cat food was a packet of pants in pastel colours. She moved the shopping in her trolley until they were hidden beneath a box of breakfast cereal.

"I have to go," she said.

"See you around," I said.

"Maybe," she said.

I watched her push her trolley down the aisle and just before she reached the corner she looked back.

Nicole Hart

The Believers

I know people who believe in ghosts. These believers are not hippies or new-agers, but lawyers and accountants. They are smart, rational people with access to the dead. When I ask them how, they tell me to stay vigilant. They say you never know when or where a ghost might appear. I met a real estate agent whose young wife died in a plane crash. Her ghost sometimes visits him when he's dining alone. He eats dinner by himself at the Olive Garden every night, just in case.

I wanted access to my dead. I searched everywhere. I wandered the aisles of CVS listening for giggles. In grocery stores, I peeked behind cereal boxes. Once, while waiting for the D train, the doors opened and a small figure hesitated at the threshold, silhouetted by the bright subway lights. There stood my little sister's loopy curls, her chubby knuckles. But as the figure walked from the train to the platform, it transformed into an old hunched woman wearing a church hat with giant purple bows.

It took nearly three years of searching. I was at a *bat mitzvah* party of all places. We had just finished the *hora*. The girl of the hour tucked the lavender dress behind her knees and sat on a chair in the middle of the dance floor, clutching the sides of the seat. Four men gripped the legs of the chair, lifting it into the air. I shifted my glance from the girl to the entwined arms of the men and then back to the girl. And what I saw was not a ghost. It was her, right there in front of me. Her face, her hands, her dangling legs – her whole self – rising towards the dimmed lights of the ceiling.

Emily Macdonald

The Prodigal of Mangamutu

The old man sits in the fraying cane chair, parked by the open front door. He sucks hard on his pipe, blows enough smoke to make it look like he's burning green gorse out on the back paddock.

When Cal pulls into the yard, Trip gives a half-hearted bark, thumps his ragged tail on the boards and yawns to his feet.

Cal cuts the Ute's engine. "Dad," he says through his teeth.

The old man cocks a trigger finger but stays framed in his chair. Cal counts how long he's been waiting by the number of beer bottles parading by his feet. Five, all as empty as Sundays in August.

"Back with ya tail between ya legs?" the old man laughs, wheezing and cracking like burn off.

"Just passin' through. Not staying." Cal says as he mounts the porch steps.

"Like last time, eh?" The old man wheezes laughter again, burn off inflamed by a sudden change of wind.

"Want another beer?"

"Na, no need now, but you go ahead son."

In the dark front passage Cal is briefly blinded after the harsh afternoon light but he strides through to the back. The kitchen lino is clean but worn, peeling away at the edges. The clock on the wall still says 6.30, like it did on the day he last left.

The fridge cool eases the heat in his face. Cheese, butter, eggs, and bacon wrapped in waxed paper sit on the top shelf. One pint of milk and Tui beer bottles fill the remaining space.

Cal cracks the crown off one beer with another, leans back, eyes closed and pours into his mouth. Pours the beer, first one then the other, like he's watering a sapling parched by the drought.

Hélène Beavan

The View

Someone once told him trees communicate with each other through their root systems. They warn one other of approaching dangers, floods, drought or disease. They get on with the business of being a tree. Humans meander through life. Do they look out for each other? Not until it's too late. Then it's the governments fault or an Act of God. The wood is speckled with brilliant light. The birch and lime trees cloak together making canopies. They bend in the breeze with the lightness of tree breath. There are trills, warbles of birdsong. He hears the distant yellow sound of the ambulance siren on its way to and from the danger zone. He thinks of his wife working in the hospital back home. He slumps on the edge of the field on to a tussock of grass surveying the two views. Behind, the wood. Before him the land of polytunnels stretches far to the horizon. He wipes his fingers on his overalls, reaches for his tobacco, rolls a cigarette. The smoke lifts on the updraft disintegrating. A wood pecker hammers insistently. He enters the trance like state of smoking and breathing, breathing and smoking. The shout goes up, it's the end of the break.

Inside the tunnel the heat is tremendous. Humid and timeless. He works quietly and skilfully. He'll exceed his quota. He thinks of nothing as he picks. He places the blooming fruit into punnets with a reverence like a priest distributing the Eucharist.

Beverley Sims

The Beast

Uncle Neil lives on *The Street in the Sky*, where the lifts are clean and shiny and all the buttons work. At the final ding me and my brother leap onto the main landing. Dad points out the Manchester Ship Canal, his voice booming like a cannon.

Mum's brother hugs her for a very long time. I think he might be famous. He wears fancy waistcoats and has hundreds of thankyou cards. He picks one off the sideboard to show Mum. *Elton*, he winks, and she suddenly starts to cry again. I sit on the squeaky sofa, pretending not to notice.

After cherry tarts Uncle Neil says, 'I've got just the ticket,' and goes to The Beast. It takes up a whole wall with its layers of gleaming white teeth and blinking eyes. He presses the pedals into the pink carpet and flicks switches, until voices wheeze from hidden throats and the room magically fills with invisible musicians and choirs and marching bands.

I wish with all my heart I was allowed to touch even one single key. Just one, to see what roar it might make. But Uncle Neil never offers and I don't dare ask.

He plays something called *Boogie Woogie* to cheer Mum up, and soon Dad is flinging her around like a rag doll, and she is laughing and crying at the same time and now I know that whatever the *Big C* is, it can't be that bad.

In the lift back down she presses her finger to her bottom eyelashes, and I try to work out how The Beast got all the way up to the top floor in this tiny lift. My brother jams his sticky fingers into every button. I don't mind. I don't want that final bump to come at all.

Katja Sass

Sisyphus with a thimble

When someone does the same thing every day, every single day, like Maggie does when she pulls up a chair at the quilting table, goes into the sewing pouch thumbed and faded by her roughened hands, removes some now-blunt pins, fixes three blue and white polka dot patches back into place and slowly sews, just as she did last night before the finished spread was unpicked again by prison guards to keep the women busy mending a perpetual but non-existent problem, making them nothing more than Sisyphus with a thimble, then eventually that repetition, that wearing down of hours, months, years, acts as a narrow plane, carving a groove into reality, making a ghost of Maggie before she even dies, where, on repeat, she pushes pins easily into an increasingly punctured fabric, so that when that final day comes, when she is packed, on her way back out into the free world, not as Maggie who sews but as the wife who pushed a knife into her husband's heart while he slept, no fresh bruises for defense, irredeemable, Maggie steps off the bed in her cell and hangs herself with material she's saved and sewn over the years, and her soul simply unpicks itself from her body, tugs at the stitches of sinew and nerve until it falls free, returns to the table, slides into the groove she has worn in, rebecomes the blurring in the seat next to the other women, with them all reaching for more pins, always.

Seamus Scanlon

Where It Counts.

In school he was brave, bombastic, hyperkinetic. He was Mensa material. He soaked up quadratic equations, recoil free fractions, prime numbers. He wore an ankle bracelet. He wore a wrist bracelet. He had blue green eyes. He had high cheek bones. A girl magnet. A boot boy target. Their steel toe capped boots never landed. Their long-leashed German Shepherds fell back. He was a balletic street fighting king. He laid them down on the wet Galway streets. He delivered round house kicks. He slashed cheeks. He broke femurs. He was a black eagle falling through a flock of doves.

He broke girl's hearts. They trashed around him like fish breathing their last in the bottom of a currach. They scooped up his body. Their pale white Irish skins vibrating with untold sins. They swopped bracelets. They swopped breaths.

At dusk, on one of those long languid summer evenings you sometimes get in late August, he was walking across the roof ridge of McCambridge's in Shop Street. He looked down at me. He stumbled slightly. But righted himself. But then gradually he began to slide down the pale blue slates, slick from an evening mist rising off the Corrib. We all watched. Cars stopped. Cyclists dismounted and looked up. On Shop Street all was calm. All was quiet. He did not cry out. I did not look away. His pelvis shattered. The noise was incredible. Leg bones pancaked. The ragged stems of femurs jutted through his beautiful skin. The broken eagle.

Surgeons worked on him for days without end. For months I stayed beside his bed in Merlin Park. Visitors looked askance at me. I nodded at them – the Galway bear hug. He cried on the long nights. I cried myself but inside where it counts.

JR Fenn

The Cherry Tree

We moved to a small city by the Great Lakes from another country. The cherry tree in the front yard bloomed not long after we moved in. That winter, a storm split the trunk.

It has to come down, the tree guy said. As he turned to leave: So, where are you all from?

I'd picked up an accent from my years of living in the country of my husband's birth. I pretended to hear my daughter inside.

A few weeks later, the truck pulled up. The door opened. A silver crutch stuck out.

A tree fell on me, he said. Shattered my leg.

Are you sure you want to go ahead?

The crew cut off the branches, sectioned the base. A bulldozer dug out the roots and carried them across the sky in torn-apart chunks.

What about the hole? I said. It gaped, a crater between the house and the street.

What about it?

You said you'd fill it in.

After they'd gone, I found the contract in a pile of papers. *When we remove the beautiful tree from your yard, we pledge to fill up the hole, smooth it over, seed grass, leave it as if the tree never was.*

I called the tree company. They sent a crew to fill in the hole.

A truck began driving past the house.

The telephone rang. Hello? my husband said.

Go back where you came from, the voice said.

Late at night, there was a knock. We hid in the dark. A rain of pebbles exploded against the house's face. A truck started up, puttered off. After that, we didn't see the truck again. Grass grew over the spot where the tree had been, as though it had never been there to bloom, or be ruined, or taken away.

Roberta Beary

Cactus Stream of Consciousness at Earthly Paradise Retirement Centre

The cleaner's spritzing me with a bottle that says organic I hate the cold wet feel of it I have to wait to get dry because no one here lifts a finger to see how I'm doing since the hospice nurse left no one ever asks are you okay Granny O'Donnell read in the New York Times that we should check in on each other more loneliness is coming for us all that cleaner woman is still here her name tag says Sally I wish I could tell Sally to move me into the sunlight on the windowsill and use her feather duster silky soft feathers on my succulent spikes would feel heavenly Sally tosses the bottle into the recycling bin she stares into my cactus finery and says listen up this place is hell on earth a dog couldn't live on what they pay me I want to tell her it's Earthly Paradise and also what's a dog but she's thumping me in her cart saying no one will miss me but I know Granny will Sally tells me to say a final farewell turns her cart around so I can see no Granny no pink sheets no blue and white crocheted afghan Granny said I reminded her of the four green fields of home but she didn't even say goodbye Sally lifts her feather duster and brushes me lightly her big hands push the cleaning cart towards the exit sign's blinking red lights I'm crying cactus tears and

James Borley

Platinum Plus

Stevie liked to scream at the car wash. It was private and dark and if she chose the Platinum Plus option it would last almost 8 minutes, which was usually all she needed. She loved the feeling of the giant metal frame moving over the car, its arms never quite touching. Reiki by machine. She'd put the car in park, push her seat back and wait. The pre-soak would start and the world would fall away, obscured behind thick sheets of water and soap. It felt like being swallowed.

When she was a little girl, her dad always washed by hand, claiming the machines would damage the paintwork and encourage rust. Each Sunday he'd wash the car on the drive whilst Stevie watched from her bedroom window. She took the car when she left for university. He reasoned that she'd need it more than he would. *Just keep it clean*, is all he said to her. She thinks of him sometimes, when she's in the car alone, not quite ready to go home.

The first time she screamed, she laughed straight after. All that energy bouncing around the inside of her car with nowhere to go, like electrons circling. It was the day after her dad's funeral. She had stopped for petrol, bought a lottery ticket and – on impulse – a Gold Wash. She cried at first. Her tears felt insignificant, diluted, but then the scream found its feet, just as high pressure jets surrounded the car, matching her pitch and cancelling her out.

Sometimes she buys two washes simultaneously and wonders, on the second lap, whether the water will ever get in, needle its way underneath, breach the rubber seal, strip the paintwork and let the rust set in.

Mamie Willoughby Pound

Lucille

Cattle-brown cardigan buttoned at her collar bone, page boy hairdo, streaked through with grey. Tom is fifteen inches taller than she and wears a nervous black leather belt, three inches in width, hung with keys that rattle-rattle as he sniffs, shrugs his shoulders and explains the merits of safety belts in his Lincoln Continental. We wriggle in short shorts with long, long hair, too young for braces even but still understand Granny when she says her sister Lucille is still made to do it with Tom, well into her sixties and how Granny is secure in her own Pepto Pink bedroom, swags and cascades above every window, always shut tight. Tom's Lincoln is Lake Martin green, murky and cool. Seat fabric like a thin summer t-shirt and smells like Lucille's ashtray and her Avon Lemon Cold Cream. Backseat wide like a twin bed. He never puts that car in reverse until we snap click on the seat belt, its cross-guard ribbon between our breasts. Once just to be funny we unclicked on the way down the steep driveway and he no lie put it in park, car frozen perpendicular to the street below. Backseat higher than the front seat. He put one finger up and turned to remind us again, but before he could get going, Lucille said, Oh, Tom.

Carol Ann Parchewsky

The Trichologist's Lament

An average person loses one hundred hairs a day and they grow back. I don't remember when mine stopped growing back or when I first counted sixty-seven hairs when I brushed out the snarls of nightmares of confrontation and conflict before my shower or when I counted thirty-three hairs when I combed in the soothing avocado-scented conditioner that promised lustrous regrowth and the ability to multitask and macromanage and the strength to blossom and over-achieve under a micromanager from hell. I do remember the one hundred-seventy-two hairs that clogged the vacuum cleaner beater bar as I tried to vacuum the spilt flour from the middle child's 'forgotten until the absolute last moment' science project attempt on the day that the house was going on the market, and I had a 'do not be late super important' presentation at eight across town. I remember changing my part from left to right and then deep right. I remember watching the reel about the efficacy of hair toppers again and again and again as I waited for the tow-truck. I don't remember why I thought the light was green. I don't remember what the micromanager said first when she sandwiched that I was fired in with did I do something different with my hair and did I see that viral reel with Heather Locklear and what was that scrumptious perfume. An average person is fired at least once. An over-achiever is fired at least once on their birthday. An over-achiever finds every hair they lose after they lose their job and an over-achiever creates their own wig based on a YouTube tutorial.

Jonathan Peters

Post Vital

Sam sat in a cold, red folding chair on the front porch of his apartment, facing the parking lot, partially shaded by stairs. Every hour, a deep, metallic breath echoed through his open window. The sound came from a grandfather clock in his home, a relic from someone he used to know.

Sam wore a white leather mask with silver spikes jutting out of the cheeks, and bronzed, bug-eyed goggles. He bought them for Halloween two years ago, but never wore them until now. He looked ridiculous.

A police siren slipped through the night, red and blue strobe lights probing the parking lot of Sam's apartment complex, responding to reported gunshots fired into the night blue sky.

Sam was daydreaming, floating through the blue-green methane comfort of a Neptune world, melting into the nothing-mist. He was flushed awake when the clock death-rattled one last breath upon the back of his neck, the police car now stopped directly in front of his apartment, lights scanning the darkness for violence.

Sam was racing to a screaming red light, as he absently-mindedly stroked the barrel of his silver .38 caliber revolver, like it was his tortoiseshell cat, Luna. He'd been redlining all his life, driven by the alarm bells of rage.

Sam stared darkly into the probing lights, then loaded a round into the chamber of his .38, waiting for the metallic gong to rest in peace.

He was God of this methane world. The God of bells.

Sheri Reynolds

The Chiropractor's Birthday Party

Once upon a time, ages ago, someone threw a party for the chiropractor.

The grown-ups had their cake in a long green trailer. The children splashed around in the pool, and Silver wore blow-up donuts on her arms, pushed up above the elbows. Holding out her arms, kicking her feet, she could twirl and twirl while her mama and the chiropractor boogied between lounge chairs, behind the prickly hedges, and back inside the trailer where they stayed a long, long time.

She met two girls named Tammy and Tina who wore whipped cream on their noses to keep the sun from burning them off.

Now, sometimes at night when it's lonely and the crickets gobble up her dreams, she closes her eyes and remembers the green trailer, the pool surrounded by the chain link fence, the smells of chlorine, cigarettes, butter cream, twirling in the pool all day and night, falling asleep in the water with floaties on her arms.

What a feeling, to wake up bobbing beneath the sliding board.

Her mama was passed out in a lounge chair, wearing nothing but her sideways party hat. The chiropractor snored beside her in his Fruit of the Looms.

Somebody gave Silver a swim ring. Somebody brought her Doritos for breakfast. She ate them in the pool. By the time her mama woke, the soggy ones had floated off to China.

Now that her mama's in rehab, Silver recites her memories: dizzy circles in the water, chattering teeth, the beach towel with a map of Florida that somebody threw over her mama.

Somewhere you can buy waterproof whipped cream just for your nose. Somewhere, two girls named Tammy and Tina twirl all night.

They're out there even now, somewhere, twirling right this minute.

Don't forget.

Tom O'Brien

Skeuomorph

Mother and Father face each other, each in a separate room. Mother curls round a book in her favourite chair, looking past words with newly revealed meaning. Father runs his finger along the imperfections on the kitchen table, tracing a crack that goes to the edge.

Back from school, the son stands trapped in the hallway's angle, looking through one door, then the other. He lifts his hand-me-down phone, which has little power and no credit, but the camera works. What he wants is a picture of them in one frame, to capture what can't be seen, to hold some kind of proof.

He taps the illusion of a button, afraid pressing too hard will break it. He looks at the image, scrubs his finger on the wall between them, but the division remains concrete.

The son whispers to the face reflected on the toughened glass, telling that boy to stop crying, but that's the boy who hears the silent arguments, the boy who reads the language of absence and distance, so that's the boy who cries, but quietly. He can't let go but he can't hold on.

The phone falls from the son's hand, cracking on the cold floor. Two heads snap back from private futures, to see there is only now in their child. They rush to him and wrap their arms around his trembling body, around each other, oblivious to whose touch soothes who.

The son's eyes search the floor for the shattered phone, willing that boy to take a picture, so he can show them all what this looks like, and what this looks like can become what it is.

Rachel Maloney

Epilogue for Baldwin IV of Jerusalem

It was spring when they carried him across the desert in a litter. By then the dying king was so ill that his body seeped into the white linen, in a yellow oil that reeked of herring gone to rot. They hadn't the resources to replace bedding at the rate his body wept, so to disguise it along the road to Kerak they repurposed one of the carmine carriage covers as a sling.

I have heard the embalmer asked an unthinkable price to even touch the body; that in the time that passed between the negotiation and the exchange of coin, the body had reached a wretched state beyond imagining. The Holy King was no longer clearly man or woman—only a swelled, strange form, bloating towards heaven.

Furthermore, I am sure the embalmer is a fine man, to his fellow men. As a servant, it is not my place to suggest my fellow maids take care to not be caught alone with him—perhaps the fault is mine for fetching water alone. A few minutes of pain, my skirt slung up over my back like a saddle rug, and it was done.

I remain employed, so long as I am quiet. I cured and smoked my disquiet like meat.

Three months since and there is a steady swelling now, festering under my skin. I pray for our late king often, as I sweep, tend, vomit.

At night while Jerusalem sleeps, it is as if I am on that litter with him, our entwined immobilized bodies trundling towards some fate that God did not mind reusing.

Hana Gammon

Cow Tools

Look! lowed the mother to her shaggy-haired child, t*hese are the fields where our ancestors grazed*. The calf flicked his tail and was silent. If he had a name, it would be something like *post-anthropocenic ungulate* or *New World Aurochs*. But there was nothing left now with the power or desire to name. Names no longer mattered. Not to the child. Not to the mother. Not to the expanse of blackened topsoil stretching out before them, riddled with old spinal columns and the crumbling remains of concrete pens. New growth spiralled out of the middens, tangles of dandelion and nettle, good for grazing. At the foot of one mound there lay a skull, almost engulfed in green. The calf had seen such skulls before, scattered about like chaff. Flat-faced, hornless, with delicate jaws and tiny peg-teeth. When questioned once how such a feeble animal could protect or even feed itself, his mother had simply explained that it couldn't. Not on its own.

Our ancestors must have been very kind, the calf thought, meeting the empty gaze of the unfortunate creature, *to have shared their world with those who hungered most.*

Audrey Niven

Chips

There's a turn in the stairs where you can't be seen from the floor above or the floor below. A half landing, if you like. The ideal place to make yourself invisible.

I tuck myself in on the half landing between seven and eight. We live on six. If anyone's looking for me, they'll automatically look down. That's the escape route. I'm safe up here.

He went down like a sack of spuds. It was comical.

'I'll have you,' he said, glowering at me. 'I'll fucking have you.'

I took him out with the chip pan. Didn't know I had the strength. My hand reached behind me like a reflex, took hold of the handle and swung. His head smashed off the corner of the cooker and landed in a halo of peelings. I burst out laughing. There was oil everywhere and not a mark on me. I still had the knife in my hand from cutting the chips. I never used it on him, but I wrapped it in a dishtowel and flung it down the bin chute on my way up the stairs just in case. Don't want anybody getting any ideas.

What I'll do is, I'll go back down and I'll phone the ambulance and tell them I just came home and found him there like that. Quite handy that he banged his head. I'll say I came home thinking he'd be hungry for his tea and there he was, drunk on the floor. Knocked himself out, I'll say. Stupid fucker doesn't even know how to make chips, I'll say. And they won't argue.

Unless he's conscious. If he's conscious, the game's up.

Colm Larkin

Country Roads

When her glaring full beams showed a rare straight on the tight and twisted country road, Marie stomped on the accelerator. She snapped a finger to turn on the radio, hoping to drown out the broiling in her brain.

"...a stupendous strike and from 2-0 down, it's now 3-2. What a turn—"

Marie thumbed a button to change the station. She hated football – the one thing she had in common with her mother. The image of that woman lying in bed, with only the gleamy malice of her pale blue eyes piercing the gloom, brought Marie's fury to a boil again. She tuned back into the radio.

"...by John Denver. Next up, we're heading to 1983 and Total Eclipse o—"

Marie skipped stations again to a tumultuous assault of syncopated beats. A voice, from a generation as distant to her as she felt to her mother, spoke

"This is 180FM and youse have all been axing: can I get a rew—"

Marie slammed on the brakes, pounded the radio's off button, jerked the car around and drove back through a smug silence.

The old woman growled as Marie opened the bedroom door.

"I thought you'd stormed out. Couldn't even see that through."

"Jesus Christ mum, you never change."

"I'm dying Marie, what's the point?"

Marie reached for her mother's thin hands.

"What made you come back?" asked the woman.

"The radio," sighed Marie. "It was even more infuriating company than you."

"I'm glad you did."

The woman pressed on Marie's hand and 40 years of slights and sneers, shouts and slaps, disgust and denigration hung in the room, a toxic transmission that had soundtracked their life. Its noise would not abate with her mother, but for now, Marie was content not to tune in.

Lucy Mac

Cornered

I shouldn't have cheated.

Alcohol-fuelled weakness that I hoped I could pretend never happened. But I'd overlooked one significant detail: a witch's sense of smell, like her sense of justice, is spellbindingly strong.

I'd forgotten Elvira's stories of the days of volcanic darkness when no light perforated the sulphur dust. Where blinded witches found each other by scent, waiting out the cloud to see the moon anew together.

Elvira smelled the other witch on me and retaliated by trapping me within a postage stamp.

My God, though, how she licked my back, slowly, tantalisingly, softly. Before she pushed down hard on my front, sealing me to my fate: a cream, wax-sealed, tissue-lined envelope.

Cornered, she thumbed my frozen face, and I quivered motionless.

From my two-dimensional, recumbent position, I stared at the fullness of her. Below the waves of the stamp's bottom edge, my pining, negated body still tingled with uncanny realness.

She posted me into the gloom, to send me across the world.

Blocking out the pitiful cries from the other incarcerated souls I landed upon, I looked within and forced myself to read her letter inside:

I've made you as small as I feel. As flat. As dull. Your worth printed for all to see, as it has been on me.

For the last time, I gaze upon your profile. Basking in the pixels of light on your monochrome face.

I inhale you. I want you. I hate you. I love you.

She *still* loves me.

I recognised my final chance to repent.

My tears trailed to the address where I swirled new cursive letters out of an ocean of regret. The price on my head was all but spent. My ink bled dry. Until, at last, I saw beneath me those three little words:

Return to sender.

Jennifer Lane

The Gap

Hannah grips the base of the pram and shuts her eyes, preparing for the shock of pain as she lifts. Up, and over the gap she's supposed to 'mind', but which is so frickin' wide even Babar the elephant could slip through. The pram is heavy, too heavy, and Hannah feels like she's been run over by a steamroller, whatever the hell a steamroller is. Her stomach, a sick rainbow of purple, blue, brown, yellow. Three fractured ribs, her pot of gold. But she can't think about that now. Focus on the positive.

Ella's finally put on weight, that's why the effort of lifting her is sucking the breath out of Hannah. Ella's no longer 'failing to thrive', no longer a loser before she's even learnt the alphabet.

The rubber wheels hit the train floor. They're still bouncing when Hannah's phone buzzes against her thigh. Hands instinctively let go, just for the teensiest bit of a second.

Has he checked the wardrobe?

She doesn't look at her phone, doesn't even reach for her pocket, but the damage is done. In an instant the doors swoosh shut and the thick, breath-smeared glass slices her world in two: Hannah on one side, Ella on the other. Hannah throws her broken body against it.

The train lurches. The carriages groan and screech. Hannah slaps and kicks at the cold glass. It's no longer the door. It's windows, faces, eyes. A man's eyebrows standing up in alarm. The honk shatters her eardrums, seeps into every bruise in her body. A kid's sneaker on the tracks. McDonald's wrappers, shattered beer bottles. The stench of a small, dead animal. The wheels are thundering. The little train that could. You bet it could. It's fast. Faster than her. As fast as *him*.

Sarp Sozdinler

'Naders

A photographer asks me to look into the camera and think about the first happy moment I can recall.

There's a time and place where some of my favorite memories as a kid are stored, and in all of them, in a dreamlike fashion, I'm cramped in the backseat of Dad's baby-blue Ford Bronco, bookended by my sister and her plush moose, watching Mom fiddle with the stereo on the passenger seat, and listening to Cher lament over a long-lost lover.

The more I try to remember the more the colors on her face crystallize into geometrical shapes, then zoom back into oddly chiseled features: her snorkel of a nose, her rosy cheekbones, her plummy lips curling to the vocals hissing out of the stereo.

What I recall next is a moose popping out of nowhere on the other side of our flyspecked windshield, and my sister's screams severing the membrane of the car's sanity. Then comes the screeching of metal dragging across the hot tarmac, followed by the almighty mess of blood and fur and god-knows-what-else on our windshield and front bumper.

Despite all its grit and grime, I remember the day proving to be a cheerful one, at least for me. For it was the first time in so long we were doing something together as a family, even if it meant doing perfectly nothing.

Despite all its grit and grime, the longer we idled by the freeway that day, the more ferociously the wind swept the litter away, flushed the tumbleweed into the air, and whirred a distant Ferris wheel like a weathervane. Even then I could sense Mother Nature was trying to claim what was once Hers. That was probably why She first perished the moose that day and let the rest of us watch it.

Sara Hills

Great Tits

I'm on the phone with my sister Wendy, distracted by the songbirds standing sentry on the uppermost branches of my beech hedgerow while Wendy goes on and on about her tits.

The beeches, still heavy with the paper-dry droop of last year's leaves, slump brown against the greening of April and its emergent blooms — milk-white plums and blushing cherries, even against the gold-dappled beds where daffodils lift their yolky faces to follow the sun. It's as if the beeches insist on clinging to the past long after the rest of the world has woken up.

Twenty years ago, Wendy reminds me, flashing her tits gained us entry into a VIP nightclub. Only ten years ago they fed her babies, Drew and Elise.

The chatter-song of the birds calls me closer to the window, and I search the hedgerow for signs of renewal, google the absence of beech budding, until Wendy reveals the results of her latest mammogram: a proliferative spot still fairly small, its cells clumped like grains of pollen.

For the first time, I worry about needing a tree surgeon; imagine the growl of a chainsaw, the deep pitted holes, the garden wall a blank canvas. Exposed.

As if sensing some danger, the sentry birds lift off and away. And when I ask what she needs, I almost feel Wendy's shoulders rise in response.

I can't say for sure what kinds of birds they were, probably common house sparrows. But later, at the hospital, I'll recount the vision and tell Wendy they were nobler ones — *Cyanistes caeruleus* or *Parus major* — glorious tits. And I'll distract her with bird names and the budding times of trees, tell her about the beeches with their marcescence, that stubborn-willed way they keep holding on.

Karen Arnold

When My Skin Became Paper.

The first time, I thought the edges of my skin would unfurl, simply roll up and away from the thin blade of ink like a snapped tendon. I was an anomaly in the tattoo parlour with my office clothes and steel grey bob, perched on a scuffed black leather seat, beneath the flash sheets and price lists.

A pierced sylph of a girl bent over my arm; jet black hair pulled back from a fairy tale white face. She conjured a humming bird from my wrist, blue as her latex gloves. She wiped away the blood as I wiped away my tears and sent me out into the sunshine, to stand dizzy and amazed by the carnival of traffic streaming along the arterial road out of the city.

It became easier after that. When he left for the final time, a death's head hawk moth landed, soft as a last breath on my bicep. A thimble after you kissed me for the first time. Galaxies of stars and planets across my belly for the children.

The bird girl left. Another took her place, wrote a life story in ink across shoulders and breasts, onto the broad blank canvas of my back. Mistletoe and ferns, bats and toadstools, an owl for the day my mother died alone in a hospital bed before I could reach her. Ivy leaves twined around a caesarean scar, an image of the Cailleach below a missing breast.

Now I move through the world like a Yakuza, inked from neck to wrists below my white blouse, my middle-aged clothes, my silver hair. A story written in permanent marker, hidden in plain sight.

Louise G Cole

Wolfie, Woodie and Red Get High at Grandma's

Little Red has been hard at work baking, and now she's running late. But when she calls for an Uber to Grandma's, she doesn't realise she's in earshot of Wolfie and he's listening carefully.

He's a handsome devil, but not her type and she's already turned him down three times this week. Four times last week.

Wolfie has decided she needs a lesson in manners. The anticipation excites – he hasn't felt this turned on since he helped Prince with all those naked feet and that glass slipper.

"Postcodes are so specific," Wolfie says, flashing a big-toothed grin when he arrives at Grandma's and she opens the door to let him in. In no time, she's charmed by his persuasive smile and agrees to sit in the pantry, confused when she hears the key turn. Wolfie goes around switching off lights and closing curtains.

"Grandma, it's awfully dark in here," Red says when she arrives minutes later to sit on the edge of the bed.

She doesn't hear Grandma's reply since she's locked in the larder. Instead, there's a sudden scuffle as Woodie joins them, equally eager to try it on with the gorgeous Red. He's been following her for weeks.

She turns on the light and is surprised to see what big eyes Wolfie has, what big … hands Woodie has.

She knows what to do. "I have Brownies," she says. "Pain relief for poor Grandma, you know?"

They do know.

Soon, they are discussing time travel, polyamorous throuples, the cosmos, and a You Tube video she's watched about castration using only copper wire, tweezers and a screwdriver.

Wolfie and Woodie agree to try therapy first.

Carefully balancing the plate with the last of the brownies, Red goes to find Grandma and make them all a cup of tea.

Jane McKie

Casting Out

She smells of newsprint that collects in the lounge in ridiculous piles. She often smells of fragrant tobacco. Today, she smells of a fish supper and I know that tomorrow it'll be different again.

As hauntings go, it's relatively mild. Once in a while, I might catch a flicker of her in a mirror, or spot whiteness coalescing in a corner. That's usually when I'm in a bad mood. I wonder if she's trying to come through more strongly to comfort me, but perhaps that's just wishful thinking.

Really, I know this is as much as I'm getting. It hasn't changed since she's been gone: she's mostly a scent – the newspapers, the fish, the liquorice. The hair dye, the shoe polish, the laundry boiling on the ring.

I've been to see a medium, who told me that someone called 'Betty' or 'Bette' or 'Elizabeth' was close. Those names aren't hers. The medium was an unreliable narrator.

When I go to bed and can't fall asleep, I worry I've trapped her in my grief. I picture grief as a sticky net, one that adheres to every surface in what used to be – still is – her house. If there's a heaven, maybe she can't reach it because I'm tying her to earth. In those moments, while I still ache, I want nothing more than for her to be free.

I think of all the smells that remind me of her – the ones I've experienced since she went and the ones I haven't yet encountered. I'll wait for the day when she smells of damp curtains stored in a box in the attic (a little bit plughole, a little bit pepper) so I can unfurl her, let her lie on the lawn while the sun burns her off and she rises like mist.

Emily Macdonald

Regretting the narrow path over the wide field

He's crossing O'Hare's yellow field when his heart is insulted. Dizziness comes first. Pain, then nausea like he's fallen foul of a virus, an amoeba or parasite in last night's left-out-for-him cold dinner.

When he falls in the wheat, the husky heads bow. They lean towards him as if acknowledging the insult is grievous. Worthy of notice. Worthy of pause.

He marvels at their close interest; basks in the attention he's shied from all his long life.

He lies, clutching his chest. His breathing is dusty and harsh. It's painfully clear that the insult is personal as if his reticence, his withdrawal from any difficulty or blighting trouble, has harvested spite, and in this moment, he knows himself to have been foolish in pursuing solitude from within married life.

While waiting for his years to flash past, all he can see are cruising carrion birds and the whiskery wheat gossiping, bobbing their ashen blonde heads, crowding his narrow view of summer blue sky.

Nicole Love

Supernova on a String

He hates the supernova in her left eye that appeared–out of nowhere– in the eternity and milliseconds after his fist bounced off her face.

The oil slick that spoils the pristine waters of her sclera and creeps into her iris like a clown's balloon floating across a cloudless sky.

The firework on her gaze that explodes into his consciousness whenever it drifts towards him. Her eyes, wide, like a child's on Bastille Day holding a doll with buttons sewn into its face that he knows he can't touch until the dust and pyrotechnics sink back into the darkness for fear of causing a scene.

The wax stamp on his summons. The ink stain on his Sunday best. The gavel banging down each and every blink of her eye.

He hates the thing that's every man's worst nightmare until the moment passes and the thing is gone–finally–after all this time, and he's in the clearing. Only one week left of thick foundation that lets the cracks seep through, until the bruises run away from her face, until she slaps a smile on.

Srilatha Rajagopal

When They Tell You to Baby a Rock

"I AM NOT THE PROBLEM."

Your announcement at Sumi's valaikappu/baby shower causes Sumi's mom to drop the bangles, *yellowmediumvioletsmallredbig*, the chattering of women dying down in waves, a patti who asks "What did she say?" shushed loudly. The pregnant silence that follows is punctuated by the clink of a falling bangle.

Your mother-in-law drags you to all the pregnancy-baby-related functions, as if you'll catch a pregnancy like a cold.

As always, you smile as they stack bangles on Sumi's hands. You smile when mother-in-law laments to her friend Shanta about the sins she must have committed to suffer this grandchild-less existence. You smile when elderly mamis ask, age their license to bulldoze boundaries, "Any good news?"

You smile but inside you scream "Ask Ramesh!!"

Because you just found out the problem was Ramesh, when you had been carrying around the word maladi, barren. Ramesh who reluctantly agreed to get tested after your results came back normal.

Because you found the photo of a younger girl your mother-in-law left carelessly, or intentionally, in plain sight right before coming to the function.

The maid's pitying look make your insides tremble, palms sweat, icy-cold. For the first time, you doubt Ramesh's love. You even doubt your normal test results. Would he remarry?

You're still in this dissociated state when some elderly ladies make you sit in the manai, place a baby-sized-rock on your lap, tell you to pretend it's a baby, sing to it, it will shame your womb into action.

The absurdity of it hits when you try to pick up the rock-baby.

You push it off amidst gasps of horror. You slip a few bangles on Sumi's wrists and walk out, but not before finishing your announcement.

"IT'S RAMESH. HIS SEMEN COUNT IS ZERO."

Your uterus whispers "That's my girl."

Marie Gethins

Whensoever

He left home for the first-time at age 84. When the coal bucket was overfull at half. When he wasn't sure if he had shaved that morning. When his footsteps on the wooden floor became less *thunk-tap* and more *schush-schush*. When his brother's wife decided she'd had enough of his advice.

He discovered peanut butter at $84\frac{1}{4}$ years old. When the attendant served a soft sandwich called 'PB and J'. When Sophia's grandchildren visited on Saturdays and offered him their home-baked cookies. When he heard the squeak of a cabinet opening in Sophia's room late one night and investigated. His slippers whispered across hall lino. When he raised his walking stick ready to strike an intruder, her trill of laughter invited him to share a stash of peanut butter and crackers.

He was a bachelor until $84\frac{2}{3}$. When the heart that his sister-in-law called 'stone' and the GP called 'weak' became something else. A *thump-thump* that pounded in time to Sophia's Big Band favourites. A swell in his chest when she squeezed his hand in the Common Room. A flutter when Sophia's lips pressed against his loose cheek.

Judy Birkbeck

To whom belongs the land?

Back end of summer, Buzzard called a parley of raptors: Ey-up, he said. Tonight let's get all grouse on Walshaw Moor, dump their bodies in bogs, then what-ho folk won't mither us again.

Ay, said Kestrel. Ay, said Merlin.

Everyone agreed: No more, do owt to help. With folded wings, perched on ground, they looked small and harmless, a circle in perfect symmetry.

I'll be your eyes, said Owl.

I'm squeamish, said Red Kite. I'd rather eat a corpse.

Me too, said Buzzard, but fear not, our Peregrine from Malham Cove's a rabid killer.

Hang on a minute. Merlin spoke up. A whole grouse? I'd be stuffed.

Who says we have to eat them? said Buzzard, head high. He wa' proud of this action he'd taken.

They even messaged Peregrines at York Minster, and Hen Harrier from way up north. Magpie heard and came full lick, preening shiny feathers. All night they slaved in rain while dawn, soaring, swooping, sunshine-yellow talons outstretched. Night sky wa' crammed with swishing wings. Peregrines hacked and gobbled. Red Kite threw up.

'Tis our own county now, they cheered.

When it faired up and blathering classes sallied forth, rigwelted grouse littered moor. Bracken wa' scarlet. Guns bawled.

R. C. Barajas

Rough Cut

Every diamond cutter you know wears cowboy boots—as if their work requires wrangling. White smocks make them look like rodeo pharmacists. You tap a ring round on your steel mandrel and accidentally knock a diamond loose, send it shooting toward the polishing wheels. As you crawl along the floor, Devon pulls on his cigarette, squinting. He suggests kneepads, and invites you to service him down under while he brillianteers the facets of a 2.4 carat marquise. Carl and Keith clap him on the back like he's already had you. He dogs you back to your bench where his oil-smeared apron ignites as your torch springs to white-hot life, oxygen cranked to melt platinum. It chases him around the workshop, crisping his flesh, rendering him a roaring fireball that engulfs the others. And you, lone woman, luxuriate in the warmth.

***

Where the security cameras cannot see, he leans to light his cigarette from your torch. His smock stinks of cutting compound and starch, his breath ashy despite the mints he pops all day. Out the window a woman passes, and to her retreating back he murmurs, *Heeeeeey!*, barely moving his lips. Cocking his head: *You should get a dress like that.* Positioning a ring onto your mandrel, you try tapping it round but your shaking hammer misses, making a ringing sound into the empty workshop. Carl and Keith have gone to lunch. Into your ear: *I wake up under a tent just thinking about you in a dress like that.* As he spins your chair towards him, his boots softly jangle. In the bathroom later, you see the gray fingerprints on your jaw and neck. What will the others assume? Wiping blackened hands over their white smocks, they might slap Devon on the back before grinning home to their wives.

David Mathews

Who Does He Think He Is?

'Thank you,' the woman said, 'that was kind.'

'Least I could do,' the man said.

The least, for sure. He had spent fifteen minutes trying to find something cheap, and settled for the £2 bunch of daffodils.

He had forgotten that his mother disliked yellow, but also forgotten how tactful she was in thanking for gifts. Politeness, she called it.

Two years since he had visited, even though he and she lived only 15 miles apart.

Estranged? Not really, though she had seen him only on the telly and once in court, where he had not spotted her in the public gallery. Too much playing to the reporters and the courtroom artist to be a convincing witness, she thought.

If not estranged, then what?

Her offence was to be ordinary. He did not want his followers to link him with ordinariness, God no.

His? Being a celebrity, not an expert. Her fault, she feels. Better to have praised him less for being a good-looking child, and encouraged him to aim for something worthwhile – in medicine, say, or archaeology – or both, like that Alice whatshername with the pink hair.

Having become *#smugbugger* after his court performance, he wonders if anybody in his family history might get him onto that ancestor show. Shit, if he could be moved to tears by someone who had been heroic in a war or roguish in peacetime, he might even come across a bit humble.

But problem: after the hiatus, how to probe his lineage without seeming barefaced?

As she arranged the daffs, the woman thought how her son was becoming like her grandfather, whom everyone thought wonderful until vanity betrayed his transgressions.

But you can't come straight out with that, can you? Instead, 'Nice touch of spring,' she said.

Deborah Tomkins

Genetically-modified colonials returning to take our jobs

There's a young one on the platform. She stands over seven feet tall in her patch of sun, her green skin glowing, bones fragile, limbs like spiders' legs. She's doing this weird thing, moving her upper body like she's restless.

Well, we're all restless. Nobody gets too close. I'm a metre away. People say there's a distinctive smell although I can't detect anything from here.

She's swaying from the hips, back and forth, side to side. I glance over, discreetly. Ah, headphones. Music. Some people claim to like it, go to clubs to get the authentic experience. Virtue-signalling, imo.

She's rippling her back now, waggling her head, her unnerving yellow eyes closed, the lids conifer-green. Make-up? Kidney disease? They suffer side effects, I've heard, something to do with the chlorophyll.

Her bare shoulders gleam, are visibly darkening in the sun. Seriously, if she stood in a wood naked you'd never see her.

They should have stayed on their own planet. Yes, they're cheap to run, don't need much food or clothing, are happy with bunk beds in dormitories. But I'd rather have white or brown or black lawyers, teachers, doctors, surgeons, engineers – not green ones, even with IQs of 200-plus. Especially telepathic.

Train's here. In the rush, I trip, fall at greenie's feet, graze my knees. People shove past, nobody stops. I gaze at greenie's orthopaedic trainers, think briefly of the gravitational stresses on her body, imagine her growing tall like a daffodil in the thin Martian air.

Long green hands grasp mine, gently raise me. I look up into golden eyes. Golden music fills my head. Gentleness fills my heart. Happiness fills my soul. We smile. We smile and dance, just us, two girls on a railway platform in the rush hour.

Philippa Bowe

Things I Did and Didn't Do Today

I didn't cry. I didn't open the cupboard and stare at your Moomin mug. I didn't trawl through the Facebook messages telling me what a lovely person my sister was, how they would miss her, am I okay? I didn't find new and clever ways to avoid the back door pile of mud-stiffened trousers and backpacks and hiking boots, two pairs, same size.

I didn't uncork the wine on the stroke of midday. I didn't lie on the sofa stroking the ratty fur of your rabbit and my badger, as soft as the day they sugar-coated our exile to boarding school. I didn't end up on the rug watching reruns on my eyelid screen, watching the rocks shift and crumble, watching you disappear like an evil magician's trick.

I didn't empty my gut of Chardonnay and toast down the toilet. I didn't slam the door shut on *life goes on, sweetheart*. I didn't wish I was tumbling down the mountain with you. Over and over. Holding hands. Touching beloved fingers and nails and curving palm lines, familiar as my own, until we landed in pieces together at the bottom.

Instead, I did scream. I did kick the bedroom wall like it was the mountain that broke you until my toenails buckled. I did let the rage in, let it blow through my head until a door opened and a tiny sliver of sunbeam crept inside. I did feel better. I did hate myself for feeling better. I did feel your fingers pinching my arm, right on the spot you used to lightly twist whenever I did anything stupid. I did get dressed, put on the orange stripy skirt you always tried to steal off me, tie the laces on my favourite trainers. Today, I did keep my footing.

Susanna Roland

Robot Nurse

My ovaries were removed by a robot yesterday with technical precision and modern-day wizardry.

In recovery, they pumped hot air under my blanket and morphine into my veins.

I waited outside for my sister to arrive and take on the role of my convalescent nurse.

In a drug-induced haze, I redirected her when she called hysterically from the wrong hospital and helped her up as she fell flat on her face, rushing to avoid a parking ticket.

At home, I mopped up the wine that leaked from her bag as she plonked it on the kitchen chair, red seeping into the cushion beneath like blood.

I listened to her chatter as she chopped and scraped, cooking up a storm of comfort food, creamy fish pie, crumble and custard, wrapping me in sisterly love.

Then I heard the clatter of cutlery hitting the floor as she opened the broken drawer with the DO NOT OPEN sign.

After dinner, it was time for her to give me my blood-thinning injection.

I watched her eyes flit over the instructions as she pointed to something on the telly.

I recalled her once poking herself in the eye whilst putting in a contact lens, flooding the white with thin red veins, and I longed for my robot, imagining the mechanical arm expertly plunging the syringe in and out in the blink of an eye.

All done, she whispered, intersecting my frazzled thoughts.

As she tucked me in bed, my belly full of soul food and stitches stretched from our giggling, she tenderly squeezed my hand.

The touch was warm and fleshy, not the cold claw of a machine.

I whispered thank you through teary eyes as she left – forgetting to turn out the light – and I concluded that Robots had neither feelings nor ADHD.

Nicola Caroli

Leech Therapy

The leech attached to the inside of my calf has involuntarily sucked into the hematic memory of the opioid-induced numbness of my birth. The leech has fallen asleep.

"That's never happened in my entire naturopath career, a leech falling asleep on a patient," Angela says, giggling. She prods the leech to wake him or her up. More giggling. I like Angela. She's larger than life, like my mother. I make an appointment with her once a year to remember I had a mother. We would lie on the narrow massage tables side by side, the leeches sticking to our bodies, my mother's reddish-brown lipstick tracing her generous mouth out of which burst short sighs, giggles and declarations of love for her predatory saviours. "I love you", "I just love you", etc. The delightful sensation of their smooth, muscular bodies, their mouths with three tiny jaws gripping her flesh, ingesting the viscous blood thickening in her vessels that is killing her, slowly, definitively.

"Such a relief!" The leeches performing an involuntary kindness – the salivating, chomping kind – that gives the blood a rush, injects vitality into the stuff of life. My mother's blood, the only flow I needed, the strongest pulse I knew before it ebbed away.

Tracy Fells

The Constancy of Woodpigeons

From the patio, Louise can hear her mobile, volume set to max, trilling inside the house. She looks up to the platform of twigs in the climbing rose that frames the kitchen window. Here sits the Woodpigeon, her serene profile clearly visible from below.

Only weeks before, John had laughed at the pigeon's mate, flying into the rose with sticks double his width, presented like a proud Labrador returning with booty from the woods. More often than not, these ended up on the flagstones. "Enough to build a log-cabin," joked John. He read out a piece from his newspaper, on how Woodpigeons could recognise and remember human faces. "They know they're safe with us," he said. "Onto a good thing, with onsite pool facilities and all-you-can-eat seed buffet." It was true; their garden, intentionally designed for wildlife, even welcomed the foxes and Sparrowhawks who often brought death to its sanctuary.

Louise risks a glance through the window, watching her eldest son, pen poised over John's daily crossword, all the boxes blank, as he takes the call. If Ben turns around, she will know whether it's good news, or the worst, from her son's face.

The pigeons are a partnership, taking turns on the eggs, and it's only Louise's whimsy believing the female is up there. Today the Woodpigeon's mate is absent, not squatting on the fence as usual. Louise hopes he's hiding near-by, waiting for her to leave before bringing food to the nest. She whispers a prayer that the fresh flurry of white belly feathers, scattered over the lawn, belong to some other overnight victim. Within the house, her mobile lies abandoned on the newspaper. Ben has moved out of sight. Like a da Vinci Madonna the Woodpigeon waits in quiet contemplation.

The patio door clicks open.

Ashleigh Adams

The Good Girls

We crept up driveways on balmy summer evenings smelling like soil and sweat and Sun-Ripened Raspberry body spray. We felt wild in the woods, safe to shed the plasticky veneer of gated subdivisions, of Methodist youth groups we attended to flirt with boys, of babysitting jobs we took so we could watch Cinemax After Dark on big screen TVs. We ate Oreos slathered with peanut butter and shared scavenged Marlboro Lights, passing them between dirt-crusted fingers until the filters tasted like Dr. Pepper lip balm. We screamed feral into the trees, sang about going down on boys in theaters, but we didn't do that, exactly, because we weren't *sluts*, we were good girls who laid plaid blankets on pine needles and made them go down on us instead. We sat at dining room tables, finishing plates of pot roast and mashed potatoes with trails of dried saliva on the insides of our thighs, and our mothers who didn't have jobs except for making pot roast and mashed potatoes said how lucky they were to have girls like us – smart girls who made smart decisions, who read books and did chores without complaining. We loaded dishwashers and swore we'd never be like them, these mothers who did nothing but wait for their husbands and make themselves small. *We are the good girls*, we thought, *we're different, we're special.* We fell asleep under Titanic posters, tucked into T-shirt sheets with kisses on our foreheads, knowing we were right.

Nick Havergal

Blue-Eyed Boy

I drive up there and the sky's porridge-grey. The nicer screws herd you out the back like a chastened cat, then they nod and sink back inside.

No Mum? you ask, right off the bat.

Your stuff's in a bin bag. *She didn't want to come up here again, bud.*

You tilt your head. A canine tooth's missing. *Why not?*

She didn't want to, I say.

We head off, the high-chained fences lumbering above us, and it's not long before you ask for a go in the car. We turn off at a junction. You stall and stumble and fumble the clutch but I see that stupid smile's back.

Donuts, Dad? You whoop and grip the wheel. I touch your arm, my grin curled like a comma, and tell you to *get fucked*.

We make it back to town as dusk blots the clouds. The sign reads 'Please drive carefully' and your shoulders snap towards the sun roof. You see one of the family's in the chippy, deadened by the lightbox menu, and you drag your hood across your brow and we're already gone.

We get back to an empty house. Mum's left for Grambo's. You perch on the edge of the couch, primed to run, leg hairs snaking from holey joggers.

We tap on tinnies, one two three, and pluck them open together. *Peas in a pod*, you say. You smirk as foam plumes from the can.

I ask you to repeat.

We're like – nah. Don't worry, Dad.

Later, you amble upstairs. You dive onto the airbed for a freshly fretful kip. I lie next to you as your nieces bloom from a frame on the desk, and I listen. I listen to you, finally, knowing so well the fits and starts in your breath.

Seamus Scanlon

Don't Go

Ma is beside me at the open front door, grasping my hand.

"Don't go Victor."

She is smoking a Sweet Afton and crying. Her two superpowers. Since my father fell off the roof of MacCambridge's Fine Foods in Shop Street during a robbery she was never the same. Nor was I. I saw the whole thing. I was looking up at him as he slowly slid down the steep granite-slate roof tiles. A sudden shower in off the Atlantic on that high summer day created an oily patina. Physics took over. He went over. Four stories.

****

I look over her shoulder. Dawn is coming.

The grey crooked streets are shrouded in fog that drifted in all night from Galway Bay.

My brother's Opel Vectra idles at the roadside.

Exhaust vapours taint the air.

The car radio is a low hum.

He sits on the bonnet looking at us.

"Victor, you nearly killed me, you know?", Ma says.

We both nearly died on the birth stirrup-line. Cord around neck. Fetal distress. Scalpel. Blood spray on the ceiling. Gush. Gush. Gush.

"I know Ma."

"This is no time to be leaving me now, you know?"

"I know, Ma."

"You don't know anything so you don't."

"No Ma, I mean yes Ma."

"How will I manage?"

"Sid." I point at him. He is doing press-ups now against the bonnet. "That brother of yours is pure mental so he is."

She grasps me tighter for several seconds.

She hesitates. Then whispers, "Victor. I'm sorry. I didn't mean all that about you almost killing me. You know?"

"I know Ma." I didn't.

She kisses me on the cheek. A first.
I escape and walk down the path.
"Make sure you come back to me," she calls after me.
I nod.
But I never did.

Owen Townend

Girls in Real Time

Guys, I stepped away from the monitor today. It was lunchtime and my fridge was empty. I had to leave my apartment.

Not long into my midday forage, I saw them. Four girls out in the open. It's been well over a year since I saw one in real time.

These four weren't peddling photo opportunities or playing games, they were just on their phones and vaping by some bushes.

I'd say only two of them had the looks to be online personalities, but, hell, I found them all attractive. Blonde curls. Brunette pixie cuts. So much eye shadow. Not much cleavage, though.

When they turned to look at me, I froze up. There may have also been some nervous giggling and the tiniest bit of throw-up. Still, I got my shit together. One deep breath and I reached for my wrist pad. They ran but not before I captured every one of their likenesses and reported them to the Connection Hub.

Hot as they were, those females should have been online, working. Without the incentive they bring to male productivity, the Connection Hub might grind to a halt.

That being said, I returned to my own monitor ASAP and got back to it. There was only another ten hours left of my shift anyway.

Of course, it was nice to see actual girls for once. Hopefully they haven't been sanctioned too hard and I'll see them pop up on my feed soon.

Marie Day

What Old Nicolas Never Told us in Antibes

We found the battered Ouija board in a box with things other backpackers had bought and left behind: a Swiss army knife, a Barcelona shirt, a beret adorned with the Tricolore. One night we took it to the beach, drank red wine from plastic bottles and demanded to know our future.

One ghost obliged, even flirted with us in English, said his name was Old Nicolas. He told us we'd quit waitressing at Café Jeanette, tired of long days and little pay. We'd head home and over time, budge town by town, office by office to be closer to one another. He spelled out the names of future husbands, children and pets. Even told us about Fridays on the common, how we'd wait for dark, roll onto our backs, staring at the same stars we'd danced under in France, dreaming of all the ways we'd be in each other's lives forever.

That last part must've made Old Nicolas smirk.

Wine glass in hand, I stare at the phone, waiting for your reply. It's been months. You've married the man whose name Old Nicolas spelled out. A small wedding, only family. I tell myself that's why the invite never arrived.

Mum rings, says she dreamt about that Australian boy I once dated while travelling, asks if I ever hear from him. I haven't thought about him in years and I wait for her to mention you, but she doesn't. No one does.

Somethings aren't worth mentioning I guess. Even in Antibes while he was busy telling us our futures, Old Nicolas never mentioned one of us would hold onto forever too lightly, never warned us how friendship has a heartbeat and a breath, how it can choke and drown and lie silent under the very same stars where dreams are made.

Nora Nadjarian

All Our Earthly Possessions

The things we loved, kept, hoarded. The things we won, prized, categorised, shelved, dusted. The things we listed, ticked, crossed out, colour-coded. The things we kept in files, boxes, drawers, compartments, fridges, freezers. The things we lost and pined over, latched on to, gave away. The things we sent and received, opened and sealed, waited for, saved up for, fought over, longed for, paid for. The things we stored under the bed, in the wardrobe, in the cupboard, displayed in the cabinet, left on the bedside table, shoved under the carpet. The things we found in books, bags, purses, wallets. The things we switched on, switched off, broke, mended, put away, took out, fidgeted with, admired, dismissed, discussed. The things we stepped on, the things we ran from, things we were given, were asked to return. The things we looked for, forgot about, thought about for days. The things we were told, things we weren't told, things, things we believed, things we stopped believing in. The things we carried, stopped carrying, started dropping on our clothes, on the table, at our feet, on the floor. The things which went round and round darkening the light in our head at night. The slow things, the gradual things, the things we started letting go, the things which started letting go of us. The things we most wanted, the things we least needed, the things we held onto, the things we let slip, one by one, the things, the things, until all our earthly possessions left us, as we left them.

Debra A. Daniel

Holding on for the Dearest Life

I want to paint my bedroom purple like the peel of a plum. Pink feels silly now.

In the backyard my father looks up at the fallen leaves on our roof. He looks down at me.

I ask if he'll buy brushes and buckets of smooth color. "I'll paint it," I say. "I'll climb the ladder up to the ceiling. I'm not scared."

***

My grandmother says ladders bring merciless bad luck. "I knew a girl who fell," she says, "and was paralyzed."

"My room's so small," I say. "I won't be on the ladder much. I'll tie a rope around myself like a safety belt."

My grandmother's hands swim in cloudy dishwater,, then she pulls the plug. "Now that I think of it," she says, "it was a step stool, and she died, covered in purple bruises."

***

My father climbs a ladder to clean the gutters.

"He'll plummet," my grandmother says, wringing her hands.

I stand beneath the ladder. My father climbs so high it hurts my neck to look up at him.

"Come down," I say. "You'll fall and die."

"You'd be better off," he says, tossing down clumps of damp, rotting leaves.

I hold onto the ladder for dearest life.

"You'd get insurance money," he says. A branch drops into my grandmother's flowerbed, snapping the stem of a dark purple iris.

He drags the ladder over and climbs up again.

***

We paint my room. My grandmother tugs her chair into the doorway so she can worry closer.

Color overcomes me. "Delicious," I say. "Good enough to drink."

"Drinking paint dries your throat. I knew a girl whose throat crusted and it collapsed."

My father holds onto the ladder so I can reach the highest places. The little girl pink disappears, and purple deepens my walls.

Debbi Voisey

The Ritual

Every night Kevin and I burst bubbles in the kitchen. He's not here physically. But in spirit, and in my mind.

Before we burst them, we give them names – *there goes Annabel; look how high Benjamin is* – and we chase and touch them, and they disintegrate like half-formed ideas.

I fill the washing-up bowl. Water splashes onto my skin, scalding me, reminding me I'm alive, even if I don't feel I am. And even if Kevin isn't.

Halfway through the fill, I grab the washing-up liquid. It doesn't smell the same as it used to; Kevin had noticed that and hated that it had changed. Why mess with something that doesn't need messing with, he'd ask. He got more like that, towards the end. Questioning things. Moaning.

I squeeze the green liquid into the water, my thumb squashing the baby on the front of the bottle. I'd once asked Kevin if he regretted never having children. He'd said no, but sometimes I watched him with his nephew; the way he played with him, told him how rockets and aeroplanes worked. And I wondered…

With the bottle of detergent upright, I squeeze, and a thousand tiny bubbles fill the room. Each one is an entity, rainbow-coloured and delicate as a butterfly's wings.

Do *I* regret not having children? I don't think so. How can you regret something you've no control over? And Kevin's gone so it's too late. But we still do the routine. We dance together, bursting fairy bubbles on our fingers, elbows, noses. Laughing, and my laugh is louder than Kevin's. Because I'm alone.

I watch all those tiny bubble-lives dance before exploding into millions of beings that never were. Lives we never created. Lives we never watched develop and float and burst into a billion micro-pops of energy.

Jeanette Lowe

Weatherman

'Cold snap coming!'

Tomaz doesn't look like a meteorologist – untucked shirt, saggy string-belted trousers – and nobody coming along the pavement even glances at the sky. Had his wife been around she wouldn't have let him out in a string belt, but they parted company soon after Rob didn't come back from his holiday.

Today Tomaz goes out early. Same cafe, bacon stench, window seat, steaming tea. Everyone's quiet. He's stopped trying to warn them, they're only interested in what's on their ketchupy plates. He looks outside. A boy stops, puts his nose to the glass. Pulls a face. Laugh if you like, it won't help.

Before he hefts open the front door of the house he scans the garden, concreted over for cars. Frost tonight, they'll be scraping screens in the morning. Cardboard across them would do it.

He opens his bedsit door. Nothing's changed. Blinds down, fridge covered with postcards, blue skies and beaches. Rob never invited him along. Didn't want him banging on about the weather. After the last postcard, after Tomaz spent days glued to the news warning about the Greek heatwave, the phone-call came. Missing. They booked a plane, stood in the dust under the tree where someone said they'd seen him.

He takes down the postcard, tea-ringed. *You'd hate it here, Dad, too hot. Me, I can't get enough of it.*

He fills the kettle, wondering about Rob's body. A crevice, a lake, who knows? Anger rises. An umbrella, a water bottle, a charged phone? How hard is it? I mean, forty-three degrees.

He opens the blind. The nose to the glass. There has to be a future, some kind of future. Tomaz takes down the postcards, puts them in a drawer. He'll make them look up. The kids. Make them see what's coming.

Karen Whitelaw

Wings

I'm carving my name into the timber floor with a pen-knife one of Mum's boyfriends left and there's a knock on our front door. The door swings open because the lock's broke and a lady's straddling the hole in the veranda like a sheriff in a shoot-out. She mouths, 'Oops.'

Mum sees her and goes all giggly. She did that too, when two heavies bashed in our door last year. The tall one dragged me kicking into the back yard and chucked me on the shed roof. I grabbed the tin edge so tight it cut my fingers, and my eyes were squeezed shut so I didn't accidently look down. Then his voice went soft, and he said he had a little girl my age, but I didn't open my eyes. Not even when his mate called him and I screamed, 'Don't go,' and they cracked up. Not until I felt his rough hands around my waist and my bare feet safely on the dirt.

Inside, Mum was leaning over the sink spitting blood.

'Piss off,' she yelled at me.

Mum invites the lady inside for a cuppa and fills the kettle. I stay on the floor, pretending I'm not watching.

'I'm Gracie. What's your name?' the lady asks me.

'Ferris.' She blinks, but doesn't snigger like most people do.

Gracie grabs the teapot off the top shelf, 'Let me help,'

Mum screams, 'No,' but the lid's already off the white packets I'm not allowed to touch.

Gracie picks me up from the home to visit Mum every week. She calls me Ferry. The first time I hear it wrong and tell her I don't have wings. She strokes my back. 'You do, you know.'

And something shifts deep inside me like I'm making room for them.

Jomil Ebro

Ill-Prepared For Both Kinds of Love

after I held you in that shivering amphibious stage, and after an invisible thread pulled your mouth into a smile as you dreamt in a stadium of a crib, and after I learned how to use the baby harness, I had you face the world because it quickens the cycle of learning, and after you waddled into mom's Speech Pathology Department—in your neon-blue frog costume and tiny red Chucks, asking for treats while the women croaked with glee—and after you asked how frogs can live in two worlds, I bobbed you to sleep as it hailed in August, and after your mom started her career while translating the phonetics of an affair, and after building your bed, I moved out, and in the new swampy apartment a mile away, I ate cold turkey on U-Haul boxes, and after Uncle Jim invited me to hang with his family and wrote a card so that I had something to open, and after hearing fireworks on New Year's Eve, you said it sounded like the infinity war in *Avengers*, and after I read you to sleep, you curled like a comma in your floor-bed of shirts, and then I ran a bath in the dark, drank a thick tempranillo, felt my ribs unspool, thought of leaving you not just to your mom's Triassic skin, but to an earth with one less harness, but after dangling over the tub with knife-tides turning inside, self-worth like the Epsom we rinse on the run, you startled me when you opened the door, biofluorescent, slumbersome, and asked, "Where'd you go, dada," rubbing your eyes, and I said quietly, "Went to war, sweetie," and you said, "When will the war end?," and I said, "When I tuck you back in," and I stepped on land.

Nick Havergal

The Last Cooper

The trussing-in starts, and now I'm the eldest, Dad's gift is a wink.

With two of his journeymen, he hammers at the hoop to fuse the staves together. The ones I listed and raised myself. The clangs ring out before the cry – *Truss-oh!* – and I'm cradled across the workshop floor, then bundled into the half-formed cask, feet first. That gorgeous smell of burning oak warms me as if it were ginger cake.

Heat and bemusement smothers the room. I clock the rack on the wall. Well-loved tools hang like snoozing bats. *The croze to cut a groove, the adze to carve a shape*. Before he went to sea, Donnie would test me on their names as I swept the floor. For penny sweets at first, then cigs to hide from Mum.

A gloop of oak shavings, yeast and Ushers beer cascades onto my head. Dad calls out – *not dreamin' 'bout motor cars now, is he boys!* – and gleeful whoops throb the walls.

My indenture is ashes by the time I wash. Hunched in the tub, a parched hand clasps my shoulder. The skin of the thumb has thickened from years at the block, with mine barely scratched.

For a second we see Don – half a second. He's drifting down to a seabed, fifty miles off Batavia, his bloodied kit dissolving away. Jetsam so precious it was claimed by the divine.

You'll keep this lark goin, Dad says. Ash tumbles from a ciggie, his Wiltshire brogue snagged in his throat. *Won't you, my boy?*

And the water round my legs bleeds black, like a baptism in oil.

Author Index